Advance Praise

the memories cascade with poignant force decades later. This unusual story surprised and moved me, especially in its tender portrayals of father and daughter, and of difficult loyalties in friendship and love— loyalties that would, as Prentiss Campbell writes, come to make what we assume about ourselves and "our small world...disappear like morning mist burning off the river."

—Eugenia Kim, author of *The Calligrapher's Daughter*

"This is sharp, vivid, and gut-wrenching story-telling of the most powerful kind."

—C.M. Mayo, author of *The Last Prince of the Mexican Empire*

THE BOWL
WITH GOLD SEAMS

A Novel

THE BOWL
WITH GOLD SEAMS

A Novel

Ellen Prentiss Campbell

Apprentice House
Loyola University Maryland
Baltimore, Maryland

First Edition

Printed in the United States of America

Paperback ISBN: 978-1-62720-099-8
E-book ISBN: 978-1-62720-100-1

Development by Laura Amortegui
Design by Luisa Beguiristain
Author Photo by Victoria Ruan

The image of the bowl, photo on cover, is that of 49.2122 Chinese bowl
decorated with parallel comb marks, 10th century, damaged and repaired with gold
lacquer in Japan, acquired by Henry Walters before 1931, located at the Walters
Art Museum in Baltimore, MD. Photo taken by Luisa Beguiristain.

Image of the Bedford Springs Hotel, translucent photo on cover, provided by the
Wikimedia Foundation.

Published by Apprentice House

Apprentice House
Loyola University Maryland
4501 N. Charles Street
Baltimore, MD 21210
410.617.5265 • 410.617.2198 (fax)
www.ApprenticeHouse.com
info@ApprenticeHouse.com

To Harold, with me at the Springs and at the firefly rocks.

Acknowledgements

Thanks are due to many fine readers including Susan Scarf Merrell, Judy Karasik, Virginia Hartman, Jody Hobbs Hesler, Katey Schultz, and friends at The Bennington Writing Seminars, The Bethesda Writers Center, and The Virginia Center for the Creative Arts. Linguist Barbara Smith Vargo's experienced eye and ear were invaluable. Gerrie Sturman of Goldfarb & Associates believed in this book. Vicki Blier, Beth Hess, my husband Harold, and my children Martha, Tim, and Rebecca Pskowski believed in me. I am grateful to the memory of my late parents, John and Nelle Campbell, who introduced my brother Don and me to the rugged beauty of the foothills of the Alleghenies in Pennsylvania, near my paternal grandfather's birthplace. There are many stories and mysteries in that region; this book was inspired by the Bedford Springs Hotel, almost a ruin as I began to write; restored and re-opened before I finished.

Contents

Prologue
April 1985

Clear Spring Friends School is rich in everything money can't buy. But sometimes, money doesn't hurt. I needed the meeting with Dick Wilson to go well.

"He's getting out of the car," I said to Sally. "Wish I'd worn my suit."

My secretary stood beside me at the window, looking down into the parking lot.

"You're fine," Sally said. "Just tuck in your shirt, Hazel." I was in my white Mexican market blouse and slacks. "Check out his bald spot."

Dick was bending over his silver Mercedes, leaning in the window. I could see his daughter, slumped in the passenger seat.

"She's in the car," I said. "So she's better."

"If she was sick," Sally said.

"Let's hope she's not pregnant," I said.

"No boyfriend."

"So?"

Dick pounded on the roof of the car.

"Poor kid," I said. "No wonder she's the way she is."

"Here he comes," said Sally. "Do you want coffee?"

"I want a drink."

"Hazel." Sally looked at me, hard. She has one blue eye, and one green, wears her long gray hair loose, doesn't use and doesn't need make up. I call her the Quaker Angel.

The fire door at the bottom of the stairs groaned open. Footsteps sounded on the stairs.

I retreated into my office. Sally and I share a suite on the second floor. The building was the dorm originally, until we built the new one. Weekday boarding for kids like Louisa is our niche market. And revenue stream.

"Good morning, Dick," I heard Sally say. "Coffee?" We go by first names here, Quaker custom. No one ever calls me Mrs. Shaw. Almost no one knows I was married briefly forty years ago, when I was just a bit older than my own high school seniors.

"No, thanks," he said, marching into my office. He didn't shake my hand, squeezed his lobbyist's expense account girth into the chair.

"Dick," I said, "We've been concerned about Louisa."

"That's why I'm here."

Again. The girl had generated trouble from her first week as a transfer last year when she accused her roommate of stealing her ring. Louisa went home for the weekend and returned wearing the ring—without apologizing to her roommate.

"I hope it's nothing serious. She's missed almost a week of classes, Dick. It's Thursday."

"I know what day it is," he said. His pale eyes were chilly and smug. He was enjoying this. *He's like this with her*, I thought.

"What is it? We want to be of help."

"Then get rid of the teacher who attacked her."

"What do you mean?" My stomach clenched.

"That black French teacher. Toto. Tutu. He groped her. Kissed her. Good thing my girl's feisty."

Jacques Thibeault, from the Ivory Coast via Columbia University, was one of my best.

"When does she say it happened?"

"It *happened* Friday. After school."

"Why didn't you tell me at once?"

"Lou was a total basket case. I put her on Valium."

Since when are you a doctor, I wanted to say. Something else to smuggle back on dorm, like the vodka. The absentee mother was in and out of rehab.

"I'm sorry to hear that, Dick."

"Not as sorry as you're going to be."

Never show a vicious dog you're afraid, my father always said.

"Dick, we're not adversaries. We both have Louisa's welfare at heart."

"Glad to hear it. When you've got rid of him, she'll be back at school."

"I need to talk to Louisa, Dick."

"No one's upsetting my little girl any more than she's already been upset."

"Sidney could be there too." Sidney's a psychiatric nurse, in charge of the infirmary.

"I'm not having her interrogated."

"Just me then. Ask her to come in."

He shot a glance at me, like a kid caught hiding someone in his room.

"I'm not parading her around," he said.

"Then let's go out. Though my office is more private." Giving him the illusion of choice.

He heaved himself out of the chair. "Don't make her cry."

Louisa sat scrunched down in the back seat, wearing sunglasses and a floppy beach hat. She's a plump, pouty brunette. Probably she favors the mother we've never met.

Dick tapped on the window. She opened the door a crack.

"I told her, baby."

I opened the door on the other side. The air was stuffy, and heavy with expensive perfume. *Opium.* She must have bathed in it. What sort of father would let a teenage daughter wear such a scent?

"May I come in?"

She didn't move.

I slid in beside her on the back seat. Dick sat in the driver's seat.

Louisa stared straight ahead, sunglasses and hat like a protective mask. There were tear tracks and smudges of black mascara on her cheeks. Her hands were knotted in her lap, hot-pink nail polish chipped and the cuticles ragged from picking.

Poor kid. I almost reached out to touch her shoulder, to console her.

"Louisa, can you tell me about it?"

"He told you." She turned away. Now all I could see was the back brim of the hat.

"I'm sorry, but I need you to tell me."

"Go ahead," Dick ordered. "How he grabbed you. Kissed you. Stuck his hand down your pants, your shirt. How you had to fight him off."

"Dick, maybe Louisa and I could chat privately."

"No one's leaving you alone with her, baby, don't worry," he said.

"Get out, Daddy."

He swiveled around. "Don't say anything if you don't want to. Like Uncle Bobby told you. My lawyer," he said to me, with a bully's smile that didn't reach his flat blue eyes.

"Just get out of the car already, Daddy. Let me get this crap over with, if you don't mind."

"Watch your mouth with me, young lady," said Dick, glowering, but getting out of the car, slamming the door. He stared in the windshield at us.

"Fuck off, Dad," she said, loudly.

He turned around and sat on the hood.

She shrugged. "What do you want to know? It's like he said."

"Louisa, to get to the bottom of this, I need you to tell me."

"Get to the bottom of this? That's great. That's great. He grabbed my ass, that's what. My tits. And stuck his tongue in my mouth."

"That sounds scary," I said.

"Disgusting is more like it, but you wouldn't know," she said. "His wife is pregnant, big as a whale. Guess he isn't getting any at home." Angelique Thibeault, a PhD candidate at Georgetown, was expecting their first child.

"Louisa, exactly when, and where?"

"He told you." Did she not want to talk about it? Was she afraid she'd get it wrong?

"Please, Louisa. What you say really matters."

"Oh, right."

"I mean it."

She took off the sun glasses. Her eyes were glassy, dull. Tranquilizers or pain?

"So I have French last period. He told me to stay after. Said he wanted to help me with the stuff I'd screwed up on the quiz. It's so noisy on dorm I can't study right."

"And then what?"

"Everyone left. He was sitting on his desk. I went up. And he grabbed me. Like I told you. Stuck his tongue in my mouth. Grabbed my tits. How much gory detail do you want? Are you getting off on this?"

Her eyes welled up. I didn't have a Kleenex.

"I'm sorry, Louisa. It's hard to talk about. Has—has anything like this ever happened before?"

"Oh, he's looked at me."

"I mean—has anyone, anyone kind of in charge, touched you?"

"He's my first pervert, if that's what you mean." She put her sunglasses back on. "So how do I get my stuff off dorm? I'm out of here."

"We are going to sort this out. There's still six weeks until graduation."

"I'm in at Sweet Briar." Her mother's alma mater. We'd never sent a kid there.

"They'll look at your final grades."

"There's a building named after my grandmother," she said, abruptly getting out of the car and slamming the door. She sat on the hood with her father.

I walked to the front of the car.

"So, you get what you needed?" Dick asked.

"I appreciate Louisa's effort."

"How do I get my things? I don't want to talk to anyone," she said.

"You don't need your stuff, baby. You'll be back as soon as he's gone. And if he's not—I'll be back. With my attorney. And we know people at the *Post*."

"I don't want it in the paper, Daddy!"

"Don't worry, baby. We're dealing with a reasonable person here, aren't we Hazel?"

The bell rang.

"Let's go, Daddy. They're changing classes." The girl jumped off the hood and into the car.

"So? What's the plan?" he demanded.

Never show a vicious dog you're afraid.

"There's a procedure we must follow, for everyone's best interest, especially your daughter's."

"I'm not interested in procedure. I'm more of an action guy."

"No one wants to prolong this. In the meantime, I'll make sure Louisa gets her assignments to work on at home."

"She's in no shape to do busy work. And she's not going to be home long. Or I'll be back. With reinforcements, if that's necessary."

Kids were crossing campus now. Louisa had huddled down so that only the top of her hat was visible. He got in his Mercedes and roared out of the parking lot. I hoped he'd hit every speed bump. Hit hard enough to damage the car, not the child.

"So," said Sally. "I've been watching from up here. Enlighten me."

"She says Jacques assaulted her. Kissed her, touched her. After class Friday."

"Jacques? No way."

"I need to talk to him. As soon as possible. Check his schedule."

Jacques came in, slender and graceful in a suit and brilliant red silk ascot. Most of my teachers wear corduroy and denim.

"Hazel?"

"I hate to say this, Jacques, but—Louisa Wilson says you assaulted her after class on Friday."

"*Mon dieu, non!*"

"I—I have to ask. Were you alone with her at all? Did anything, anything at all, happen?"

"Everyone had left," he said. "I'd handed back the quizzes in class. She'd gotten a D again. I was sitting on my desk, going over my lesson plan for Monday." He sighed. "She came back into the room. I didn't even hear her until she was right in front of me."

"And then?"

"She—she looked like she'd been crying. *Pauvre petite,* I thought. She asked if she could re-take the quiz. No one re-takes my quizzes, it's just the policy. I told her not to worry, there was time to improve."

He stopped. His eyes focused on a distant point behind me, as though he was looking through the wall of my office back to Friday's classroom.

"And then?"

"I felt sorry for her. I touched her shoulder. Just consolation, you know? Like this," he said, and reached out. His fingers were light and glancing. I caught a whiff of palm oil. "And I said to her, *Ne t'inquiète pas.*"

"And then?" My Geiger counter for trouble was ticking.

"Please, I resign."

"Jacques—I trust you—but for the girl's sake, and yours, I must know every detail. I'm sorry."

He looked at me now. "She kissed my hand," he said. "I pushed her away. She left. And that's all. I swear."

"Why didn't you tell me, Jacques?"

"I was ashamed. I—I thought perhaps it was my fault."

I almost groaned. "Things happen, Jacques. But you should have told me."

"Yes. Angelique said so. Hazel, I resign."

"No. I want you here. But—this is difficult. Her father—her father is angry. And she, she's a very troubled girl."

"Please, I resign."

"No. Now, back to class. Don't speak of this to anyone. I'll keep you informed."

"I tell Angelique everything," he said.

"No one else."

He strode out of my office, tall and dignified.

I poured a cup of coffee. *Touch the Future! Teach!* my mug said. Maybe I'd have a new batch of mugs made. *Teach! But don't Touch!*

"So?" asked Sally.

I told her.

"I believe him, Sally. But—I'm sorry for her, and I'm frightened.

It's a mess."

"That poor, sad child is a mess," said Sally. "You're right, to believe him."

"He should never have touched her. And he should have told me."

"Yes. But he did. And he didn't tell you. You can see why." She looked at me with that asymmetrical gaze, one eye green and one blue.

"I have to call Abel now. He's going to want a meeting of the Trustees Committee tonight. Could you check the calendar and see if the library's available?"

"It's not," she said. "The P.A. has it."

Of course, I'd forgotten about the Parents Association monthly meeting. Sally carries our calendar in her head as well as keeping it on her desk.

"My house, then," I said. The Trustees Committee, the executive committee of the Board, six Weighty Friends as they're called, easily fit into my living room.

I reached Abel West, Clerk of the Board, at his office at the Clear Spring Bank, the bank his great-great grandparents founded. The family estate where he lives was a station on the Underground Railway.

"Oh, Hazel," he sighed when I'd told him. "The Committee has to meet right away."

"My house, tonight. 7:30. Sally will call them."

"You believe him?" he asked, one more time.

"He made a foolish mistake, not telling me. But I know my teachers, Abel. And I know my kids. I'm sorry for her, but she's always in the middle of something and it's never her fault."

"I trust your judgment. We've been through a lot together. We'll get through this."

Abel's the best Clerk of the Board I could ever hope for, and the best friend. When his wife died three years ago after her battle with cancer, I shared with him that I had been widowed, too. I told him that long ago, my young husband, my high school sweetheart, had gone off to World War II and never returned. And I told Abel's boys that my father had died, when I was about their age. But I didn't say I understood how Abel or his sons felt. In my experience, no one can. Even though loss and grief are universal, each experience is particular and unique. *You got to walk that lonesome valley, you got to go there by yourself*, as the spiritual my kids sing in chorus goes.

While Sally was calling the Trustees, I walked over to the infirmary to talk to Sidney. We're fortunate, having a nurse and counselor in one—good for the budget and the kids. Sidney coaches the girls lacrosse team. She's young, stocky, and strong. The kids like her though some believe she can x-ray their minds. Sidney cleans wounds and listens with the same fierce attention she displays on the field. She's tender, though, with the needy ones. Louisa had been a frequent caller at the infirmary.

"Whew," Sidney said after I finished, running her hands through her short, curly hair as though trying to clear her thoughts. "Starved for affection, Hazel. She doesn't read cues. Can't, really. In here, heartbroken, every other week."

"My gut says—Jacques is telling the truth."

Sidney nodded. "No way to know for sure, but I think you're right. I can see her having a crush on him. And he and Angelique— they stand out. It can make someone lonely a little jealous." She had an uncharacteristically wistful look.

"I know. Birds of paradise among us doves. Do we—do we have to report it?" I asked.

"I'll run it by CPS as a hypothetical," she said. "She's eighteen, thank goodness."

"How did she do in the Life Skills class?" Sidney teaches Health. Holes and Poles, the kids call it.

"Never took it," said Sidney. "She wasn't here sophomore year. But it wouldn't make a difference, with this, Hazel. It's not like swimming lessons, drown-proofing." All my kids have to pass a swim test before they graduate.

"I shouldn't say this, Sidney. I'm sorry for her but—I wish to god we'd never laid eyes on her. I wish her father had withdrawn her last semester, when I suspended her for the plagiarism."

"What do you know about why she transferred here?"

"Social problems. And he needed the five-day boarding what with travel and—well, the mother. The grades were so-so. She was a gamble, but Clear Spring is all about the second chance. We had that space to fill on dorm, after Emily left." And Dick Wilson paid full freight, I didn't need to say.

"What kind of social problems?"

"Vague."

Back in the office, I called my colleague Anne, the headmistress at Louisa's prior school in Virginia horse country. My friend Ted, headmaster of another Quaker school, says all heads of schools live by a code of thieves honor. We borrow from each other, we steal from each other, and we pay our debts to each other. I had taken Louisa off Anne's hands. She owed me.

"So," I said to her. "Off the record. If I told you that a certain student I took as a transfer from you last year accused a teacher of assaulting her, would you be surprised?"

"Well, Hazel, you know we can never predict that sort of thing. Not what happens, certainly not what someone says."

"Right. But sometimes it's a total surprise, and sometimes not."

"Let's just say, off the record, this is one where I wouldn't be totally surprised."

I hung up the phone. Maybe I should have read harder between the lines of Anne's lukewarm reference for Louisa eighteen months back.

Ted says there are things only another Head can understand. It would have been good to hear him say not to kick myself. But there was no way to reach him, already en route from his school in the Hudson River Valley to tomorrow's annual conference for the Heads of Quaker schools in Washington. If the Trustees' meeting tonight didn't go too late, I could still make it downtown and spend the night with him. Without traffic, Clear Spring is less than an hour away from D.C.

Ted says running a high school is like running a crisis center. You have to be able to focus and compartmentalize. I powered through two days work in one, preparing to be out of the office at the conference. Sally brought lunch to my desk. I didn't feel like being in the cafeteria with the kids. And at the end of the day, she shooed me out.

"Go home," she said. "Rest before they come. Have something to eat. Not just these cookies at the meeting." She gave me the tray of snicker doodles, brownies, and chocolate chip cookies from the school cook. "Call me when it's over, let me know how it goes. And if there's anything you need me to do tomorrow, while you're at the conference."

"Maybe I shouldn't go," I said.

"You should go," she said. "It will help to get away."

"What did I do with the agenda for tomorrow?" I started to sift through the piles of paper on my desk. She put a cool, firm hand on mine.

"It's in your briefcase."

I walked home across campus. The fields had just been mowed. The fragrance of fresh cut grass filled the air. The sun was low, striking the apple blossoms in the orchard at the edge of the school property. Our land is our treasure. A local Quaker gave her family farm to the Founder of the school thirty years ago, when he had his vision and announced to the Meeting that Clear Spring needed a school.

Developers have wooed us. We've managed to hold out.

I called Ted at the Shoreham.

"Where are you? I have a gorgeous room—looks right into Rock Creek Park." His school, Maplewood Friends, can provide a good expense account.

"Emergency meeting with Abel and the committee. I'll come, it may be late."

"What's up?"

"Tell you later. Abel will be here soon."

My mother's clock on the mantelpiece struck seven. I keep things simple—no pets, no plants; two hundred and fifty kids are enough to take care of, but I wind her clock once a week. It keeps me company. Sitting on the window seat, with a tumbler of bourbon, I looked out across the pond to the cluster of small one-story ramblers, faculty housing. Jacques and Angelique would be there having dinner. The couple rarely ate in the cafeteria. Some faculty live off-campus to avoid the fishbowl, but on-campus housing is a valuable perk in this area. I lived in an apartment on dorm, when I first came here to teach history at the brand new school twenty-five years ago. The head's house is larger than the rest, set apart—an embarrassment of space for a single woman. It has heart of pine floors, built-in cabinets and book shelves. Our Founder was a cabinet maker.

The front door opened. We don't lock here. "Hazel?"

"I'm back here!" Abel came in, loosening his tie.

"Offer you a drink?" School events are dry, but private is private. He shook his head.

"Sidney checked. We don't have to report it to Child Protective Services," I said.

"That's good, I guess. I'd rather handle this in-house."

We went into the kitchen. I plugged in the coffee urn, uncovered the cookies. Abel carried the tray into the living room, nibbling a snicker doodle.

"I have bread and some good cheese, Abel." He's a tall man, and gaunt since his wife's death.

"Thanks, but I'm not really hungry."

"I called her former headmistress today. Something similar may have happened there. I'm kicking myself."

"We were down a kid. What's done is done. Now we just have to work through what's best to do for the school," he said.

"We have to back Jacques," I said.

"Hazel? Am I too early?" It was Maggie Stadler, the newest member of the committee. Her eldest daughter was a senior this year, bound for Swarthmore. Maggie's the oncologist who took care of Abel's wife. She came into the room, put down her knitting basket, unwrapped her shawl, and gave us both a quick hug. If I ever have cancer, I'm calling her.

By 7:30 the committee had gathered: each in our accustomed seats, like a family gathering around a table. I always take the captain's chair, one of those the Founder made. It's un-cushioned, and I'm thin so it's a little uncomfortable, but that keeps me awake.

Abel was in the wing chair by the fireplace. "Good evening, friends. A moment of silence, please."

We follow Quaker procedure for business meetings—*Faith and Practice*, not *Roberts Rules*. We open and close with silence. Listen to each other and for the voice within.

"Thank you for gathering on such short notice. Hazel will explain. We have a most concerning situation," Abel said.

It was so quiet in the room. The spring peepers in the pond outside were calling. I took a deep breath. I kept my eyes on Maggie, her quick hands, her flashing knitting needles. "One of my students has accused my teacher Jacques Thibeault of assaulting her."

Maggie put the knitting down in her lap, and looked at me.

"I've spoken to the girl, and to her father, and to Jacques. My counselor, Sidney, has been quite involved with the student. She transferred in last year. There have been a lot of issues."

Sam Jiles interrupted. "Have you reported it to Child Protective Services?"

"Sidney has spoken with them. At this time, it's not reportable because she's eighteen. I've also spoken with her former school. It's possible there was a similar situation."

"Then why did we take her?" said Sam. He's built like an opera singer, and is a fine baritone. He sings in the community chorus with students, faculty, members of the Meeting. He runs a non-profit, clerks my Finance Committee, and is one of my most generous donors.

"Let's hold our questions, friends, and hear Hazel out," said Abel.

"What exactly does she say happened? And what does your teacher say?" asked Dave Furbush. He's an attorney, estate planning mostly, and has handled some matters for us pro bono. His son graduated two years back, with Abel's youngest.

"The girl says he asked her to stay after class. That he kissed her, fondled her. That she ran away. Jacques says she left with the others, then came back and asked to re-take a quiz. He told her she couldn't—it's his policy—but not to worry, there would be time. He says he did touch her shoulder, out of sympathy. She kissed his hand, he pushed her away."

"He should have come to you right away," said Dave, a tense look on his face. He must be almost sixty, like me, but looks much younger.

"He should have. But I believe him."

Sam shook his head. Maggie was biting her lip.

"Her father demands I fire Jacques. He's threatening to involve an attorney, the media. Jacques has offered to resign. I have refused."

"And so, friends," said Abel, "that's where we stand. Tonight, we must thresh through this, consider our options, and discern carefully the best course for the school."

"It's just she said, he said?" asked Dave. "No witnesses?"

"It was after school on Friday. The kids are at sports."

"No other teachers at all in the building?" Dave persisted. It felt like I was being deposed, though I've known these half dozen good people and their children for years.

"The other two teachers on his hallway coach cross country. So no, no one."

"And he doesn't coach anything?" Sam asked.

"He could, if we had the money for tennis courts." My heart was beating faster.

"Friends," said Abel. "Let's not get caught in the weeds here."

"Okay," said Dave. "We must consider the best interest of the child: protecting her and all the children, if there's any chance what she's saying is true."

"I agree," I said. "And I'm worried about her. We're all about protecting the best interest of the child here. But letting her fabrication and her father's threats take down a fine teacher isn't good for her. Isn't protecting her best interest, in the long run."

"My daughter's a senior, too," said Maggie. "Only one student transferred into the class last year. So, without naming names, I know who this is. Sarah was assigned to be her First Friend." We have a buddy system for new students. "I don't, in any way, mean to blame a possible victim—but she struck me as—well, troubled. I would be very, very hesitant to rely on what she says."

"Just because she's troubled doesn't mean she's lying," said Dave.

"And you can't take her being troubled and him being a good teacher to the bank," said Sam. "Sorry, but I for one think we should accept the teacher's wise offer to resign, tie this kid in bubble wrap, get her graduated, and move on. I know who we're talking about too, and I know exactly what the Annual Fund was counting on asking for from her dad."

I was almost trembling. Stay calm, stay calm, I reminded myself.

"There's something at stake here even beyond the cost of a lawsuit, or losing a gift. Jacques is a fine teacher. And I have to say it—he's one of our only minority teachers, too. We can't sacrifice him to slander and extortion."

"This isn't about race, Hazel. This could be a game ender. To fund a suit like this might be, we'd have to sell the land. Bankrupt the school, ruin the reputation we've worked so hard to build," said Sam.

"Jacques is exactly the kind of teacher who is building that reputation! Remember my report to the Board about the new Honors seminar in Camus and Sartre? That's Jacques. With teachers like him, we're beginning to be able to offer something unique, to attract some really good students."

"Well and good. But not bankable. We're not so many years out from our reputation as a hippie haven of free love and drugs, Hazel. Perhaps that's slipped your mind," said Sam.

"Sam, Hazel. I want to be sure we have an opportunity to hear from everyone. Friends?"

Abel's gentle reproach smarted. Once in my early days as Head, I was "eldered" as we Quakers say, called to meet with the then Clerk of the Board and the Founder. *Be mindful of letting others speak,* the Clerk had said. *Measure twice and cut once,* the Founder said.

Quaker process is slow. The goal is to come to the shared "sense of the Meeting." We don't vote. We discern the Way. We seek consensus.

The clock struck ten, and then half past. The coffee was gone, only crumbs left on the cookie platter.

"I don't think the child intends harm," said Maggie. "But I don't think she's able to report accurately. Remember when the drama club did *The Crucible*? As the mother of four girls, let me just say teenage girls can be suggestible. I think we should slow this down, find a middle path. Like a leave of absence for Jacques, just till she's gone."

"My friend Maggie speaks my mind," said Dave.

Nods around the room signaled consensus. Or exhaustion.

Abel looked at me. "Hazel?"

"Friends, ordinarily I would stand aside." That's always an option, for the minority voice, rather than obstructing consensus. "But—asking Jacques to take a leave of absence is something I cannot do. It is an expression of no confidence. None of you work with him. None of you really know him the way I do. And—hiring and firing faculty are the Head's decision."

"Right," said Sam in his resonant voice, "and renewing the Head's contract is the Board's decision. In June."

Maggie looked at me, pleading or apologizing. "Could we—could we at least lay this over? Defer a decision until next week?"

"Not if he serves us with papers," said Dave.

"Not if he's bringing the media," said Sam.

"Oh, I don't think he'd do that," said Maggie. "What father would expose his daughter to media about something like this?"

Dick Wilson would, I thought.

The clock struck eleven.

"Friends," said Abel. "The hour is late. I for one am too tired to discern clearly. I suggest, if we agree, that we accept Maggie's suggestion to lay this over. Just for the weekend. I propose Hazel and I will meet with Jacques on Monday."

"Tomorrow," said Sam. "What's wrong with tomorrow?"

"I'm at the conference for Heads of Quaker schools tomorrow. And it's too late to get a substitute for Jacques. The girl's not on campus."

"First thing Monday," said Abel. "What do you say, Hazel?"

The illusion of choice.

"Very well," I said.

"This has been a thorough threshing session," said Abel. "Thank you, Friends. A moment of silence, please."

I like our Quaker expressions. 'Threshing session' conjures

images of neat bales of hay, of harvest brought home. But as I sat in the closing silence, I saw a storm-ravaged meadow.

We adjourned, without the usual chuckles and yawns. There were no cookies left for Sam to wrap up to take home to his wife, or to eat in the car.

Abel stayed behind. He loaded the mugs into the dishwasher. I dumped out the coffee; I put the urn away until our next meeting.

"Please, Hazel, discern with care," he said.

"Fire him, you mean. Or be fired."

"No. But I do want thee to weigh the options. Thee must consider accepting his resignation." Abel had never used plain Quaker speech with me.

We embraced before he left. After Linda died, people wondered about us. But I learned my lesson at my first school about falling in love with a colleague. That's why I came to Clear Spring, my own second chance. As I used to teach my students in American History, George Washington said to steer clear of entangling alliances.

After Abel was gone, I called Jacques. The lights in his house across the pond were still blazing.

"We're behind you," I said. "Abel—Abel and I want to meet with you first thing Monday morning."

"So they don't believe me. Even if they did—it's no good. I want to resign, Hazel."

"No. Please, Jacques. I want you to stay. The school needs you. We'll meet with him on Monday. At eight, in my office."

I called Sally. "Basically, they want me to accept his resignation. Course of least resistance."

"Maybe you should. There might be a lot of suffering for him and Angelique."

"Maybe Rosa Parks should have moved to the back of the bus.

Maybe William Penn should have taken off his hat to the king."

"Don't lecture me," she said. "I'm just saying I'm worried—about the girl, Jacques, Angelique. You."

"Thank you. Sorry."

"Do you need me to call Jacques?"

"I already did."

"And?"

"I told him I want him to stay. He wants to resign. We're meeting with Abel Monday morning at eight."

"Do you want me there?"

"No, thanks. Maybe I should skip the conference tomorrow."

"Go. Let this settle. Clear your mind."

I threw my things together—nightgown, toothbrush, outfit for tomorrow. Spritzed *Aliage*, perfume Ted had given me, which I never wore at school. I drove too fast down the driveway between our playing fields and hit a speed bump. My car is low slung; I'm still getting used to the extravagant red Toyota Celica. The first new car I've ever owned. Ted calls it my late mid-life crisis car. It's a bit embarrassing to park it among the Volvos at Meeting. But driving through the dark night toward Washington with the top down, I pressed the accelerator to the floor.

The carpet at the Shoreham Hotel is deep as moss, and the chandeliers sparkle. It's the grande dame of Washington hotels. We didn't need to worry about running into any of our colleagues here. No one but Ted on his Maplewood expense account could afford it. I rode the glossy wood-paneled elevator up. Ted greeted me at the door in his boxers. He's a small, compact man—a runner.

"It's good to see you, doll," he said, kissing me. He's a good kisser. "Hungry? Want room service?" he asked when we broke apart.

"I'm tired. I just want to go to bed."

"Sounds good to me," he said, and ran a finger tenderly down my face, my neck, along my clavicle.

The sheets were heavy and smooth. He gave me a massage, kneading the tight muscles in my back, lavishing attention on my buttocks. We made love.

Afterward, lying beside him, I began to cry.

"What is it?" he said. "You never cry."

"This thing at school."

"Tell me."

"I'd rather hear what's going on with you. Did Jack like Bowdoin?"

"I don't want to talk about that, either," he said with a rueful laugh. "His mother went off her meds again. Went to bed. He had to go on the visit by himself. She wouldn't do the hospital. Or day treatment. She's seeing the shrink twice a week. It's better. For now."

I met his wife once, long before Ted and I were lovers, back when we were all teachers, attending a Friends Council for Education conference.

"Your turn," he said.

"I don't want to talk about it."

"You're crying again."

I told him.

"Oh, Hazel," he said. "Shit. As if the job weren't hard enough, and then something like this blows up."

That's part of what works between us. We both get it, about the job. We sustain each other, even if it's just on the margins of our lives. I'm married to my job; he's married to his job and his wife and has had to be father and mother to Jack. We've been lovers ten years, longer than I've ever been with anyone. Years and years longer than my marriage.

"Abel wants me to take his resignation."

"Maybe you should. The kid is definitely lying?"

"I'm as sure as I can be. You know—it's that instinct thing."

"Are you sure this is worth going down with the ship?"

"You mean there's not much of a market for elderly head mistresses, if I lose the job?" Ted's five years younger than I am: fifty-five. We both know you can't do this job forever. It's a tough gig, but most days I feel like I'm doing what I was put on earth to do. I love it.

"Hazel—it's just your best interest I have in mind."

"Best interest! I'd be happy never to hear those words again." I went to the window. He came and put his arms around me.

"Come back to bed."

"Soon," I said. "Go to sleep." I stayed there for a long time, watching the car lights twinkle across the bridge over the ravine.

The next morning, we ate breakfast in bed.

"Eat hearty," Ted said. "You know it's going to be the eternal chicken salad today at Penn House."

I took his advice and enjoyed my brioche, the butter curls on ice, the coffee from a silver pot. It was good, being beside him, warm animals in a burrow. We ate; we read the *Post*, the *Times*.

"Here's a story for the kids in your seminar," he said. "Reagan's so-called peace proposal in Nicaragua."

My Peace Studies seminar is the only course I teach now. I tie history to current events.

"Mark it for me. How about seeing this, next time we can meet in the City? New Neil Simon. *Biloxi Blues*."

"What's it about?" he asked.

"Soldier on the G.I. newspaper. Guilty about how the war is helping him."

"Speaking of guilty—come here."

Afterward, we dressed.

"That a new jacket?" he asked.

"An early birthday present. The weaving teacher made it. She says when you turn sixty you have to start wearing purple." My birthday wasn't until June but the teacher (also my friend as often happens at Clear Spring) understood the approaching milestone felt significant, even a little frightening. Both my parents died young; far younger than I am. For years I have had an increasing sense of being on borrowed time; everything I do must matter. The weaving teacher's frivolous gift and fashion advice had cheered me.

"You're getting a head start on this birthday. I'd better start planning."

We shared the mirror. I did my makeup, enjoying the neat economy of his gestures as he tied his tie, fastened cuff links.

"Leave your stuff. I have the room tonight."

"I should get back."

"Tomorrow. You'll think more clearly after a break."

"Won't think at all, if I spend the night."

I gathered my things, packed my bag. I did stick to my resolve. I did not spend the night with him. But although I had no way to know it then, the conference would disrupt everything. The past was about to grab me by the throat and drag me away from the crisis at school.

We travelled separately to the conference at Penn House on Capitol Hill. I parked on C Street. I come into the city as often as I can, on field trips. Soon, we would make our annual school bus pilgrimage to see the cherry blossoms at the Tidal Basin. *Vigilantes tried to destroy these trees after Pearl Harbor,* I tell my kids in Peace Studies, *because the Japanese gave them to Mrs. Taft.*

But the trees didn't do anything wrong, someone always says.

No, but when elephants fight, the grass gets trampled.

Penn House looked shabby next to its patrician neighbors. Lilies of the valley lined the weedy brick path. The broad front door was open. Only Quakers would leave a door open here.

"Hazel," said Jane Samuels. She's the resident director of Penn House. In her perennial uniform of navy blue skirt and white blouse, she looks like a nun in street clothes. She was a nurse in Vietnam, and did jail time for pouring blood on the draft files in Catonsville.

I slipped into a seat at the long mahogany table, polished and gleaming despite stains from years of meetings. Marilyn Bartlett, head of tiny Hilleston Friends in Virginia, sat down beside me. Ted was already there, across the table.

"Good morning, friends," said Jane. "A moment of silence."

Ted bowed his head. He has thick, salt-and-pepper hair. I closed my eyes. It would be second period by now at school. How was Jacques managing?

Jane cleared her throat "So, it is my pleasure to welcome our keynote speaker. Dr. Bledsoe is on sabbatical from Oxford, teaching at George Washington University. Many of you are familiar with her research on cultural identity among children, so helpful as you include children of different nationalities in your student bodies. Please join me in welcoming her."

Polite applause greeted the speaker as she stood and moved to the podium.

She was slender, wearing a simple, expensive linen suit. Eurasian—part Japanese, I thought.

"Thank you. I am delighted to address Quaker educators, for I have experienced the kindness of Friends. As Jane said, I study the development of national identity—with a special interest in trans-national children, children with feet in two cultures." Her voice was low, the accent neither BBC nor Oxbridge. "My topic chose me, as is often the case. My mother was English, my father Japanese." She adjusted fragile, gold-rimmed glasses with small, delicate fingers. "Complicating my own question of identity, I spent the first years of my childhood in Berlin, during the war, as my father was attached to the Japanese Embassy. In 1945, we were detained in the States at the Bedford Springs Hotel, in Pennsylvania. I was thirteen."

It was like skidding onto unexpected black ice. I had known

her, known her parents. Closing my eyes, I saw a small hand waving good-bye, flickering from the rear window as a black limousine drove away down the hotel's driveway.

At the coffee break, I chatted with Marilyn and then retreated into the ladies lounge. The room was furnished with wicker and lined with age-spotted mirrors dating from when Penn House had still been a private home.

Dr. Bledsoe stepped into the room and slipped into a toilet stall. Twisting the faucet, I splashed cool water on my face and blotted it dry. She emerged and stood beside me, dusting her cheeks with powder. Our eyes met in the mirror. Hers were unchanged: almond-shaped, smoky gray-green.

"Cha-chan," I said, "Charlotte—I'm Hazel. From the Springs."

She froze.

Jane popped through the door. "Oh, here you are. Wonderful! Dr. Bledsoe, I wanted to be sure you met Hazel Shaw. Head of Clear Spring Friends—she's developed a Peace Studies course. You two should talk."

Charlotte Harada Bledsoe turned and smiled at Jane, perfectly poised. A diplomat like her father. A performer, like her mother. "Thank you. In fact, we're old friends."

"Really? What a small world it is! Find us at lunch, Hazel. You can catch up."

But at lunch, I did not eat with Charlotte. She was besieged; everyone had questions.

"You knew her when you worked there?" Ted asked softly as we stood in line for chicken salad.

I nodded.

We ate with Marilyn, balancing plates on our laps, sitting in the narrow garden behind the townhouse.

"At my school, we haven't ever had a foreign student. Unless you count the family that moved from New York," said Marilyn.

"I get the occasional U.N. kid," said Ted.

"How about you, Hazel? Diplomats' kids?" asked Marilyn.

"They go to Sidwell," I said. "We're like Avis. We try harder. I have a Republican though. How's that for cultural diversity?" Louisa Wilson, my Sweet Briar girl.

At the end of the afternoon, Jane sought me out. "Join us for dinner. Just Dr. Bledsoe and me. There's a Japanese place near the Cathedral."

The restaurant was small. The kimono-clad hostess exchanged a few words with Charlotte in Japanese, and seated us at one of the traditional low tables. The green tea hit my blood stream like elixir.

"Now how is it you two know each other?" asked Jane.

A pause. "Hazel worked at The Bedford Springs, where my family and I—stayed." Polite euphemism, *stayed*. Diplomat's daughter.

"Where is that, exactly?" Jane's eyes sparkled with gentle curiosity.

"Bedford's about half-way between here and Pittsburgh," I said.

"I'm going there tomorrow," said Charlotte. "To the Springs."

"Could I come with you?" I asked, surprising myself.

"I would like that."

Jane ordered sake. "A toast to your reunion," she said.

We touched our porcelain sake cups together.

I drove the fifteen familiar miles back to campus. Turning between the brick bollards marking the school drive, I noticed our sign had been vandalized again. *Clear Spring _ _ _ ends School*, it read. A practical joke by one of my seniors, most likely.

I called Sally. "So, how was it today? Anything more from Louisa's dad?"

"Not a peep," she said. "Try and get some rest over the weekend."

"Actually, I'm going away tomorrow. Just overnight. I met an old friend at the conference."

Sally, my Quaker Angel, sees right through things with her bi-colored eyes. She may suspect, about me and Ted. Perhaps that's why she didn't press for any details about my plans.

"Good," she said, "That's good. Try not to worry. Way will open."

"Could you tell Thomas the sign needs to be re-painted again? Wish we could figure out who's doing this, bring him to P&D." The Head, the Dean, two teachers, and two students sit on the Procedures and Discipline Committee. Louisa had been brought before us, after trying to hire another student to write a paper. The boy had totally misunderstood her request, she said. *I just meant for him to proofread, check my spelling!*

I started to pour my bourbon, but selected the unopened bottle of Suntory instead.

"I thought you didn't like whiskey," Ted had said when I bought it in Manhattan.

I retrieved something else from the very back of the cabinet, carried the small package to the table and unwrapped layers of tissue paper. The black pottery bowl had been broken and mended, the shards joined together with golden glue. The bowl's design of blossoms and Japanese characters seemed caught in a net of shining gold seams. The long-ago artisan who fused the fragments with seams of lacquer dusted with powdered gold had transformed breakage into beauty, highlighting the damage as part of the bowl's history rather than hiding its repair.

I used to display the bowl on the mantel beside my mother's clock. One year, at my Head's reception for entering students, a new parent said, "That bowl is a glorious specimen of *kintsugi*. Where ever did you get it?"

"A gift from a friend," I said.

Afterward, I had it appraised at the Freer Gallery and learned *kintsugi* was born of a serendipitous accident in the fifteenth century. A shogun sent a broken tea bowl to China for repair. Dissatisfied with the way the mending's visible staples marred his bowl, he ordered a Japanese artisan to re-break it and repair the bowl with golden glue. The fractures made a gleaming pattern and *kintsugi*—golden joinery—developed into a ceramic art form. The Gallery's estimate of the bowl's value shocked me so much that I hid it away deep in the cabinet. Really, I should have put it in my safe deposit box. Someday it could supplement my pension. Or I might leave it to Clear Spring, bequest from a dead hand, no questions, no explanations possible.

I placed the bowl on the mantle, broke the seal on the Suntory and had my drink.

Upstairs I pulled the cord in the hallway ceiling for the attic ladder. I brought down a cardboard carton and opened it. The smell of dry paper and paste reminded me of grade school, of the Bedford library on a summer's day. Like a good historian, I made neat chronological stacks of papers across my bedroom floor: recital programs, my yearbook, letters, V-Mail, newspaper clippings. A folded piece of rice paper, black ink bleeding through the translucent page. A heavy envelope from the War Department.

Primary sources connect us directly to the past, I teach my students.

Neal's photograph watched me from the bureau. Young, not much older than my boys at school. His expression was serious, his jaw set and square.

The phone rang.

"How was dinner?" Ted asked.

"Fine."

"Are you okay?"

"More or less."

"Less, it sounds like," he said. "Come back."

"I'm leaving early in the morning."

"Where are you going? I thought you had to be at school."

"To the Springs. With Charlotte Bledsoe."

"So she was one of the children?"

"Yes."

"Wow. What are the odds? Amazing."

"Yes."

"You sound strange. I miss you," he said.

"I miss you, too."

But it wasn't Ted I missed. I carried Neal's photo to my bedside table; black and white, but I saw the wheat color of his hair and the green flecks in his brown eyes. His lips were closed but I remembered how soft and warm they were, and the space between his two top teeth.

The half-remembered lament from the tenth century Japanese poet Murasaki Shikibu floated into my mind. *Why did you disappear into the sky?*

I held the picture, looking into Neal's eyes, as though the lifetime I had lived since he died, the lifetime of years between us was dissolving. Lying awake, I listened to the hours chime and stared into the shining darkness of the past.

Chapter One

Neal and I married almost straight out of high school. The war accelerated things and determined the timing, but we'd been heading there ever since we met in 1932, in the first grade at the Common School in Bedford. We claimed each other like kin and as friends long before we were sweethearts.

The Common School sat in the heart of town, across the street from the cemetery, surrounded by churches and homes, along a long alley between the Courthouse and the Jail. My father walked me to school the first morning, from the Jail where we lived: a hulking, Victorian structure that combined house and prison. To me it was just home, spacious and comfortable, with leaded stained glass in the transom above the broad front door, oak floors and wainscoting, a front parlor and a dining room, a big kitchen and a neat pantry. There were two bedrooms upstairs, his and my smaller one in the turret. Just as a New England farm house may be linked to the barn, our house connected directly to the cell block through a thick metal vault door. Every evening, my father changed out of his uniform and bathed, as though washing away the soil of the job before cooking our dinner. We lived our family life behind the triple locked steel door, separate from the cells. At Christmas, he would bring me with him into the cell block, delivering the holiday meal, cards, and gifts. Occasionally, my father took a young inmate, a raw farm boy who'd gotten into trouble, under his wing. He'd tutor him in the kitchen. I sat beside my father, absorbing the reading lesson, learning that people could do bad things without being bad people.

***

"Why can't I stay home? I know how to read," I asked the first day of school, standing at the edge of the school yard, hanging onto his warm hand. He'd braided my hair. I had on a scratchy starched dress instead of soft, well-worn overalls.

"There's more to learn," he said. "Thee will have a fine day. School is thy job now, Hazel." The building was tall and imposing, with a mansard roof above the second floor. I hesitated at the edge of the school yard, trying to hide behind my burly father, peering out at the milling children on the sloped yard in front of the school. Boys gathered acorns from the huge oak tree, a Peace Oak planted at the school at the end of World War I. They threw the acorns at each other. Girls squealed and ran back and forth along the fence line. It didn't look like fun to me.

The bell rang and suddenly the children formed two lines, girls and boys, in front of the separate entrances. My father pushed me toward the end of the girls' line, prying my fingers loose.

"Is she scared?" said a boy, a latecomer, strolling up to us instead of joining the line.

He was so skinny, the knobs of his elbows looked sharp. Scuffed shoes stuck out beneath his pants' frayed cuffs. He reminded me of the wooden clogging puppet I'd seen at the County Fair. The stiff whirls in his wheat-colored hair stuck up in random tufts, the way fields looked just after being mowed, before the grain is bundled into tidy bales. He was smiling, a broad, open grin. He was missing a front tooth. I had a missing tooth in exactly the same spot!

"Look," I said, scrunching up my lip, pointing at the gap.

"We're twins! I'm Neal Shaw, I'm six and I'm going to first grade. Who are you?" He spoke fast, the words tumbling out.

I looked up at my father.

"Introduce yourself," he said.

"I'm Hazel Miller. I'm seven. Going to first grade, too."

"Why she's so old?" he asked my father.

"My father was teaching me," I said. "Now I have to go to school."

And then the teacher was calling from the porch, "Girls and boys, girls and boys, hurry along please."

Neal shot across the yard to the tail end of the boy's line. My father kissed the top of my head and tapped my back, pushing me toward the school like a marble into a chute.

Once inside, I passed through the girls cloak room. It smelled of rainy days and a long summer's emptiness. I followed the girls into the hallway and discovered we were with the boys again. The Common School had segregated entrances by sex; a remnant from an earlier time, but inside everything was coeducational. All of the children were white. The few Negro children in town went to a separate school near the rooming houses where black chauffeurs and maids stayed while their employers vacationed at the Springs Hotel down the road.

The older, bigger children were racing up the stairs. Drowning in the hubbub, I stood stock still.

"Hi, Hazel," said the boy from outside, coming up beside me. "First grade is over there." I followed him, like a duckling imprinted on the first moving creature she sees. He became my friend, my beacon.

Neal and I were twins, in some ways. He too was an only child, and a half-orphan like me. But his father drank and would run the family hardware store into the ground before we graduated high school. Neal never knew what happened to his mother; he wasn't even sure if she had died or simply disappeared. I knew everything about my mother. Her name—Helen—began with an H, like mine. My birthday, June 30, 1925, was the day she died. Every year after cake and candles at home, my father and I took a Mason jar of violets to her grave in the Dunning's Creek Friends Meeting cemetery. Her high school graduation picture and wedding portrait stood on our mantelpiece, beside her clock. My father wound it every Sunday with a special key. Keys were a big part of our lives—the clock key, the ring of keys my father wore to lock the cells, and the doors between our house and the cells. But the front door of our house was never locked. Bedford was that kind of town.

After class ended that first day, neither Neal nor I had a mother waiting for us at home like the other children.

"You can stay after and help me if you like," said Miss Logan. A kind, intuitive teacher, helping us with her generous attention. Standing in as a surrogate mother, as other teachers would, and as I often have for my kids. All our teachers at the Common School were single women. Once married, they had to retire. We were their practice children.

Miss Logan showed us how to pound erasers against the brick wall.

Neal slammed the felt hard. His arms were long and he could reach much higher on the wall. His fingers were long, too. Spider Fingers, the kids would call him in a few years when he'd grown so fast he was lanky and lean.

We raised clouds of white dust, and sneezed and laughed and choked.

"You're a good reader," he said to me.

"It's not hard. My father showed me."

We finished the erasers and brought them in to Miss Logan. She was sitting on her desk, laughing and talking with one of the teachers from upstairs.

"Thank you, children. See you tomorrow."

I started home along the alley.

"Can I come with you?" he asked. Always, from that first day, when he asked a question, he looked at me intently. He really wanted to know what I was going to say. He stared so hard his forehead creased a little.

"I guess so," I said.

"You live here?" he said, when we reached the Jail.

"In the house part."

"Are you afraid?"

"No," I said. "My father teaches them to be better."

"Does he whip them?"

"No!" I said. "We're Quakers. My father doesn't believe in that."

"Mine does. What's a Quaker?" He fixed me with that intent curious gaze.

"We believe there's a little piece of God in everyone."

"How does it get in?"

"It's just in there, my father says."

"How does he know?" He was pure curiosity, not doubting or teasing.

"He learned in First Day School, when he was little." I told him that my father came from Philadelphia, and Quakers started Philadelphia. Quakers started all of Pennsylvania. My mother and her family were Quakers, too, from near here—Dunning's Creek, where my father and I went to Meeting, and I went to First Day School.

"What meeting?"

"Meeting for worship. You listen, to hear the still small voice inside."

"What does it say?"

"Anything. Maybe from the Bible." I took him up our front stairs and through the screen door.

"This is pretty nice, for a jail."

"It's the *house,* silly," I said.

"Who are they?" Neal asked, looking up at the photographs on the golden oak mantelpiece above our tiled fireplace.

"My mother. My grandparents," I said. "Me, in the bonnet. My grandmother is the one holding me."

"You sure have a big family."

"Not really. My mother is dead. And all the grandparents."

"So you don't have anyone. Like me."

"I have my father."

"And now you have me." I got milk from the ice box, and cookies from the ceramic jar shaped like an apple with a stem.

"These are good," he said. He'd eaten three. My father said two was enough, moderation in all things. But Neal looked so hungry and happy, pressing the crumbs on the table and licking his finger.

"My father made them."

"Does he cook for them?"

"Yes," I said. "Same as for us, just more."

I heard the sound of locking and unlocking. My father was coming through. He had to duck his head, so as not to hit the door sill. Neal looked into the dark corridor, his eyes wide again, trying to see into the cell block.

"You brought a friend home," my father said. "Looks like it's been a fine day."

"Hello, Mr. Miller," Neal said.

"You may call me John, please," said my father. He was respectful with everyone, young and old, inmate and free, but he didn't use titles: first name and last name in formal situation, but no honorifics.

His Philadelphia family included a long line of attorneys who had gone to Swarthmore. But after he graduated from the University of Pennsylvania, he wanted to run a jail—according to Quaker principles. The Way opened for him, as he said. A job opened, actually, and he came west to the foothills of the Alleghenies, to Bedford. He attended Dunning's Creek Friends Meeting, eight miles out of town, and spotted my mother his first Sunday. Her high school graduation picture and her wedding picture show clouds of dark hair, and large, watchful eyes. She was the only child of a family who had settled the valley and founded the Meeting in 1800, when western Pennsylvania was a wilderness frontier. I spent weekends and summers on my maternal grandparents' farm, until my grandfather died clearing brush when I was three. My grandmother died that same summer. The farm went to auction, and my father put the proceeds of the sale aside for me. "For Bryn Mawr College," he told me, from the beginning.

Neal stayed to supper that first night, and often, afterward. His father didn't seem to care or notice. He learned about setting the table. And my father showed him about cooking. We would talk over dinner. My father loved the pleasure of table talk, had taught me to save up morsels of my day to share. I've read about the effect of early maternal loss, and have seen it among some of my kids. But I grew up secure, taking love for granted, as all children should and the fortunate ones do. We had more than enough love to share with Neal.

My father washed the dishes, we dried. We would sit at the kitchen table and do homework after doing the dishes. Later, Neal would walk home down the hill to his house across the river. Even children with watchful parents walked everywhere, alone or with friends, then.

That very first day of school set the pattern for our eight ensuing years at the Common School. We would stay after and help our teacher decorate bulletin boards in the drafty entry hall, marking the season with construction paper leaves which gave way to Pilgrims and then snowflakes, silhouettes of Washington and his cherry tree, Lincoln and his axe. On the way home we would collect walnuts and line them up across the road to enjoy the mess created by passing cars. We lobbed snowballs at each other, and if I managed to hit him first he would drop and howl in mock pain. In spring, we would take off our shoes and socks, hike up our itchy woolen long johns, and go barefoot on tender winter-soft feet.

Kids teased us sometimes about being friends. *K-I-S-S-I-N-G! First comes love, then comes marriage, then comes baby in a baby carriage.* The teasing seemed to roll off Neal. He would just shake his head, shrug, and smile; at ease with himself, truly comfortable in his own skin. I preferred his company to that of girls. Girls were skittish about visiting a jail, and their mothers wary, too.

When I was ten, my father gave me a two wheeler, and let Neal use his bicycle. Neal had started his growth spurt by then, and his legs were long and easily reached the pedals. It took me longer to get the hang of it, to trust the balance, but with Neal's encouragement and my father's steadying hand on the bicycle seat, I finally got it. After that, our narrow valley world had no limits for us. We could bike to the Coffee Pot, a round cinder block building with convex windows, painted silver with a decorative red spout and handle. Even the line of rust dripping down the tarpaper beneath the spout was accidentally perfect, as Neal pointed out to me one day as we sat at the picnic table outside sharing a root beer. Or, on longer summer afternoons, we would cycle along Route 220, above the rushing water of Shober's Run, out to the Bedford Springs Hotel. We'd hide our bikes in the shrubs by Naugel's Mill on the edge of the resort property and hike in.

The hotel shimmered, magical as the Taj Mahal I'd read about in *National Geographic*. The main building had a white colonnaded porch and upstairs balconies decorated with gingerbread fretwork like doilies on a valentine. The golf course stretched into infinity down the narrow valley. We speculated about how rich you had to be to stay there.

We sampled the spring water and declared it stinky. Every Bedford school child knew the Indians had discovered the water, eight miraculous mineral springs. We waded in it, to test whether it would work for us. Would it soothe our bug bites, the way it had cured open sores for the Indians and the white settlers? That's why the first hotel had been built here, after all, in 1805. That's why presidents stayed here—well, not the famous ones, but Polk and Buchanan. And the first transatlantic telegram from England to America arrived here. People still called Bedford the Jewel of the Alleghenies. "I'm from Bedford, Jewel of the Alleghenies," Neal would yodel as we hiked the trails. We sneaked in to swim in Lake Caledonia. We sat in a hillside pavilion (I loved that word, *pavilion*) above the hotel and spied on guests playing croquet on the lawn below. Sometimes, in the last summer before high school, I felt a quickening in the air between us, and would look at him and catch him looking at me. We'd run then, spooked on the darkening path. We hid and ambushed each other—grabbing each other, rough-housing. He was all bone and muscle. Once, by accident, he touched my chest and we broke apart, stunned.

"Boo! I'm John Brown on the lam from Harper's Ferry!" he shouted.

"Oooo,Oooo,Oooo ... I'm the lost pioneer child come to get you!" I retorted.

Our friendship, our kinship, changed in high school. Not uncommon, I know now, for best friends—especially a girl and a boy—to grow apart in puberty. But then it was the end of my world. In the black and white graduation portrait of our eighth grade class,

I stand on the third step of the porch outside the Common School. My expression is worried, severe as though I intuit the coming changes. Neal, tallest of all the children, is on the top step, grinning, as though he anticipated his coming popularity, knew that for him the roller coaster was rising.

Neal grew into his raw-boned frame and became handsome, a rising star on the football team. He was such a good athlete; it didn't matter about his father, or that he came from the other side of the river. He travelled in a pack of admirers, boys and girls. At first he tried to include me, calling me to join them in the cafeteria, but I hung back. So we parted; no rift, just drifted apart, perhaps like twins who need to separate.

I joined the yearbook, the newspaper, the literary magazine. But for me, solitude has always been the best cure for loneliness, and I spent hours in the library, or reading on my window-seat.

"We don't see much of Neal," my father observed.

"I see him at school." Actually, I felt his presence. I didn't need to see him to feel him nearby. In class I sometimes watched him, covertly, and occasionally caught his eye on me. And at home football games, seated high on the back of the bleachers, I felt a thrill of pride when his teammates carried him around the field. And a stab of jealousy when the girls clustered around.

"I want you to have piano lessons," my father said. My mother's piano, a mahogany Chickering upright, had stood in our parlor as just a silent piece of furniture. "With Grace McKee."

Grace McKee lived alone in her family's fine Queen Anne house on Juliana Street, just two blocks from the Common School, near the Library. It was hard to judge how old she was. My father's age, about. She was pretty in a quiet way. Her hair was blond and permanent-waved. She wore cotton shirtwaist dresses she tailored herself on the treadle sewing machine upstairs, and smelled deliciously of lavender cologne. There was a designated room for everything in

Grace's house: music room, library, sewing room, dining room, and parlor. Even a small greenhouse where she grew orchids, and lilies—the conservatory, she called it. And she had attended a different sort of conservatory in Pittsburgh, to study music. I studied her house like a spy, a cultural anthropologist, sniffing the lozenges of sandalwood soap in a china saucer on the washstand, admiring the oil paintings in heavy gold frames, wading across the deep jewel-toned carpets, coveting the doll collection brought home by a missionary grandfather. She let me open the glass-fronted bookcase in the hallway where the dolls lived. My favorite was the Japanese doll with her paper-white porcelain face, four tiny silk kimonos, and four wigs. I was far too old for dolls, and had never cared for them before. But I carefully changed her kimonos, changed her wigs as the seasons passed.

Grace had cool, delicate hands. She showed me how to place my fingers on the ivory keys and how to arch my wrists. Learning to play required my complete concentration. The absorbing focus of the lessons proved an oasis. My father often came, just before the lesson ended. The front door clicked open and Grace sat even a little straighter on the piano bench beside me and touched her hair. He sat behind us in the cane bottomed rocker to listen. I played for him, and then Grace would play. She used the pedal when she played for him, and the piano responded like a different instrument from the one I'd just had my lesson on.

"Stay for dinner," she would say, and sometimes we did, eating by the light of candles in her formal dining room. Simple meals served on thin china—cold roast chicken, aspic salad—simple meals that required forethought, time and preparation in the earlier part of the day. She poured water from a crystal decanter. I let myself imagine what it might be like, if my father and Grace married, and I had one of the high-ceilinged bedrooms upstairs. She loved him, I believe, but my father was married to his job, and in some quiet way, still married to my mother. I understand how that can be.

The explosions in Pearl Harbor invaded the protected valley of Bedford my sophomore year. My father and I listened to the radio one dark Sunday in December and our cozy familiar kitchen felt cold and drafty.

The boys were galvanized, excited by the far away danger and opportunity for escape. Soon in yearbook club meetings, we were re-writing profiles for graduating seniors who had enlisted at the recruiting station in Altoona. My favorite English teacher started a knitting club and I joined. She was as good at teaching handwork as literature and we contributed miles of scarves to the war effort. We never doubted how useful they would be.

The Bedford Springs Hotel closed down, the frivolity of vacations suspended and gasoline rationed. The Keystone Naval Training School rented the hotel and The Mountain Navy came to town, to the delight of merchants and the young women and teenage girls in town. My father's friend, the editor of *The Bedford Gazette*, said the grand ballroom on the second floor was set up with tables of receiving sets, earphones, and wires for the trainee radio operators. The private dining room where President Buchanan had received the first transatlantic cable from Queen Victoria was converted into a control room for transmissions, and the lounges became classrooms for theory and typing.

The former high school football coach came out of retirement to direct athletics for the trainees—touch football, softball, and mush-ball games on the golf course, volleyball contests on the hotel lawn, ping pong tournaments. The sailors practiced hand-to-hand combat on the lawn too, according to the photo on the front page of the newspaper. Some girls took after-school jobs at the Springs. They said the hotel had un-rationed supplies of Coca-Cola for the sailors and their guests, and poolside dances and hay rides to Lake Caledonia.

There was a new feature in *The Gazette:* "The Service News." My father read it quietly, somberly. He was a convinced pacifist, and the deaths deeply troubled him. But so did the events in Europe and he said, to me and in Meeting, that it was not after all so easy to know what was right. Everyone in town followed who enlisted, who shipped overseas, who was home to "enjoy a ten-day furlough." Some boys I knew made the sort of headlines no one wants. *Missing, Now Dead; Supreme Sacrifice; Killed in Action.* By my senior year, gold stars were shining in windows along every residential street in town. Boys I had known would not return from their adventurous escape to far-away places like Burma and Nanking.

And then that spring a local disaster came. A strange light filled the night sky just before I heard the siren calling volunteers to the Fire House down the block. I ran downstairs. The bolted vault door between the kitchen and the passageway into the cell block was open. He never left it ajar.

"Dad!" I called into the dark hallway. My voice bounced off the steel walls. "There's a fire!"

"I know!" He walked toward me. "It's the high school. I'm evacuating the cells. The Fire Department needs help. My men and I are on the way. Stay here."

And I saw them, the half dozen prisoners, behind him in the dim light. That was my father's way, trusting people to do the right thing given the opportunity.

I watched him from my turret bedroom, walking with his inmates down the block to the Fire House. I watched them emerge, dressed in boots and heavy rain gear, and walk toward John Street. My father and his prisoners joined the long, losing battle to save the school on John Street.

Much later, when they came back, smudged and weary, I helped him make a vat of cocoa, and he and the men sat in our kitchen to drink it. And then he thanked them for their efforts, and locked

43

them back in their cells.

The science wing had been saved, but the rest of the building was ruined. We squeezed into the gymnasium upstairs in the Common School, one giant classroom, for the remainder of the year. Science classes were still held at the high school.

Back in the Common School, sharing the odd makeshift classroom space of the gymnasium, things changed again between me and Neal. After the fire, we fell into the habit of walking together from the Common School across the cemetery to chemistry class in the surviving wing of the high school. And on a soft spring afternoon, as we walked between the graves, the lilac buds just beginning to swell, he asked me to go with him to the senior dance.

Grace McKee made my dress—taking apart a formal of her own, with fabric scarce and rationed. She fitted and pinned as I stood in her stuffy upstairs sewing room until I grew dizzy. She came to our house to do my hair the night of the dance. Grace unrolled the rag curlers and brushed and pinned the chestnut waves. I felt like a movie star and almost did not recognize myself!

Neal and my father were waiting together in the parlor when I came downstairs, floating in the cloud of organza and tulle.

"You look beautiful," Neal said.

"You remind me of Helen," said my father. And looking at my mother's picture on the mantel, this time, I thought it might be true.

The entire town lined Juliana Street to watch the couples parade up the driveway to the Common School and then climb the stairs to the gym, decorated for the evening as a vineyard with purple balloons and green crepe paper. Our music teacher cued up records on the gramophone. *Paper Doll,* and *My Heart Tells Me.* I'd practiced dancing with Grace McKee—but found it easier to dance with Neal. It felt familiar, not strange, to be close to him as he held me and rested his chin on the top of my head and we swayed among the couples as Bing Crosby sang, softly, *May I Love You.*

Walking home that night, holding hands, we kissed in the alley between the school and the Jail. And he told me his news. He was deferring his football scholarship to Penn State. He and his best friend Joe had gone to Altoona to enlist in the Army. Joe had been turned down because of his bad leg, but Neal was going. "As soon as we graduate."

D-Day came, just days before graduation.

"Will you still be going?" I asked, hoping he'd say no.

"Yes," he said. "Of course. It's not over yet." He grinned at me, excited.

Grace McKee hosted a graduation dinner for me, and for Neal.

"Best wishes to you both, and to Neal's safe return," my father said, raising a glass of iced tea. He had neither criticized nor supported Neal's choice to enlist. "Each must follow the voice of conscience, Hazel," he had said.

The night before he left, Neal took me for dinner at the Ship Hotel. The invitation pleased me. My father and I never ate at restaurants, and the Ship had a bar—which he did not approve of. But he let us go.

Neal drove us out of town in his father's rusty pick-up, through the village of Schellsburg, up Route 30 west to the mountainside inn. The Ship had been built with a deck, and portholes for windows, and it clung to the steep slope of the mountain like a boat on a wave. Even the furniture inside was nautical. Neal dropped a nickel in the telescope at the railing beside the parking lot. We counted off the three states and seven counties promised on the plaque beside the coin-box. We ate at a window table overlooking the valley.

After dinner, back in the truck, I slid across the torn seat, almost snagging my skirt on a spring. I looked at his strong fingers with the square nails as he held the steering wheel. He smelled very faintly of sweat, but mostly of Lifebuoy soap. I wished we would never drive down from the top of the mountain, just drive further and further west.

"Want to drive up to the overlook?" he asked.

He parked by the guard rail at the Bald Mountain Overlook. Leaning on the truck, we watched the moon rise. Clouds blew in, covering the moon, filling the valley below.

"Do you think an ocean looks like that?" I asked.

"Don't know yet, I'll tell you," he said.

I shivered.

"You're cold," he said, opening the truck door and boosting me inside. We kissed. He tasted of our after-dinner peppermint. With my tongue, I found the space between his teeth. He leaned over me, and I lay back in the cramped space, eager and yearning for the weight and warmth of him—but Neal pulled away, and drove us down the mountain back to town.

He stopped at the curb beneath the Jail. The glow of my father's reading light shone through the curtain on his bedroom window.

"Joe's taking me to the station in Cumberland tomorrow. Will you come?" Neal asked.

"Yes," I said.

And we kissed good-bye for the night, a long, lingering kiss.

The next day, I sat between Joe and Neal on the drive. No one spoke as Joe drove us over the mountains, past rocky farms and orchards, to Cumberland, just beyond the Maryland border. Neal and I held hands. Too soon we descended into Cumberland, the Queen City, busy and important at the confluence of rivers and railroad lines.

We kissed on the station platform, and when the whistle blew it sounded like it was announcing the end of the world.

June 30th, my birthday, my father opened his roll top desk after the cake, before we left for our annual visit to my mother's grave with our jam jar of violets. He withdrew a small, narrow box from one of the pigeonholes. Inside, a rose gold locket on a fine chain rested on white cotton batting. I snapped it open and found a tiny print of her high school graduation portrait. My own dark eyes looked out of the tiny frame.

I had a job at the Coffee Pot for the summer, the morning shift. Crossing off days on the calendar, I counted down to Neal's furlough. He would arrive home after basic training at the end of August and then he would ship out. Soon after, I would leave for Bryn Mawr College.

I read and re-read his letters. "*Got your box of cookies and the fudge from Miss McKee. They really came in handy. I'm learning blackjack. One fellow lost $45! Don't worry, I'm careful. Yesterday we were out in the athletic field for two hours. We had to do the obstacle course. It's a low hurdle, high hurdle, an alley to run through, an eight foot barrier, a tunnel thing, and a creek to broad jump. Two guys had to be carried back to the tents. Nothing else to say now, so I'll close. Your friend, Neal.*"

I wrote back, trying to spin something interesting from my quiet routine.

The morning of August 25th I heard the news over the radio as I cut a piece of blueberry pie for a customer. The Allies were in Paris! When my shift ended, I ran home, eager to talk to my father about the news as we prepared lunch for the inmates.

I found him collapsed on the linoleum floor of the kitchen. No breath, no pulse. My father was gone. Gone suddenly, quietly, without warning. Without saying good-bye.

Mr. Pate and his son from the funeral home took him away, and his best suit, a clean shirt, and his suspenders, with leather tabs soft as gloves. I gave them one of the handkerchiefs my father always carried. He taught me to iron using the hankies: a sprinkle of water from the green glass coke bottle with the perforated cap, the easy glide over the fabric, the hiss of steam and the clean smell of hot linen.

Later, I found his glasses in the dish drainer. He always washed them before eating. For a moment I thought, he'll need these. Before I remembered.

Grace McKee took me home with her the night he died. My home is your home, she said, for as long as needs be. The Sheriff would be staying at the Jail until the new jailer arrived.

I cabled Neal the news of my father's death. He replied:

So sorry. Wish with you. Home soon. Love.

I held onto that word—love—and kept the telegram beneath my pillow.

The day of the funeral, Dunning's Creek Meeting House filled with all of Bedford. Everyone crowded in and squeezed together on the hard wooden benches. The door was open, as well as all the tall casement windows to catch any passing breeze on the hot day. I wore the white pique dress Grace had made for my high school graduation two months before, sweat seeping into the crisp fabric although I had felt cold ever since my father died.

There was the rustling and settling of the start of Meeting. Silence filled the room. Grace sat beside me, fragrant with lavender. I closed my eyes on the pressure of tears I could not shed.

I heard footsteps, a latecomer.

And then—Neal slid onto the bench beside me.

I began to cry.

"Here," whispered Neal, passing me a handkerchief.

We buried my father next to my mother, in the shadow of the tall brick meeting house, beside the corn field. Grasshoppers whirred, and birds and children called.

Neal came back to Grace McKee's. We sat all afternoon on the porch swing, as people came by to pay their respects to my father, and to wish Neal well. I felt safe sitting beside him. And a deep fatigue. The days and restless nights had blurred since my father died. I was so tired. Leaving Grace and Neal to carry the conversations, I went upstairs for a nap in the late afternoon. I slipped out of my dress and under the cool sheets, listening to the faint squeak of the porch swing chain and the murmur of Grace and Neal talking below.

I awoke, disoriented for a moment by the high ceilings, expecting to be in the walnut spool bed in my small turret room. Splashing cool water on my face revived me, and I put on a fresh cotton shirtwaist. Downstairs, I found Neal shelling peas for Grace at the kitchen table. He looked at me as I came toward the table as though I was the one coming home after a long absence.

We ate supper on the small back porch—cold fried chicken, peas and asparagus from her garden, and warm rolls. For the first time since my father had died, I was hungry and could taste the food. Neal had taken off his tie, unbuttoned the collar of his uniform shirt. I watched him swallow, and wanted to reach out and touch his lips, his neck. He looked up and caught my eye.

"Go for a walk," suggested Grace after we finished.

"We'll help you first," Neal said.

"No," she said. "Go along." Her expression was soft, and wistful. I thought of all the suppers here with my father. She wanted us to go, and she needed to be alone.

"Thank you," I said, embracing her, inhaling her lavender fragrance.

We walked down Juliana Street as dusk fell; past the houses with glowing windows, past the closed shops, down to the river where we sat on the bank listening to the water, to the desultory quacks of ducks settling in for the night. The last swallows and then bats swooped through the air, catching insects over the water. We walked back through the alleys, all the way to the Common School. There on the porch, deep in the shadows, hidden from everyone except the graves in the cemetery across the street, we held each other. I touched his face, ran my finger along his parted lips, the tiny space between his teeth. We kissed, a consoling kiss that deepened until we both pressed against each other, wanting more.

The next morning, Grace and Neal helped me pack up my father's and my household, our life, at the Jail. She wrapped my mother's dishes in the kitchen. Neal dismantled my bed upstairs, the walnut spool bed that had been my mother's. I went through the pigeon holes of my father's desk. I found his cards, his pipe and pouch of tobacco—his quiet vices. I shuffled his deck of cards, remembering his poker nights, falling asleep to the rumble of deep voices. In the morning after those card nights with the Sheriff, the Judge, the editor of *The Gazette*, I would find all the downstairs windows open—my father airing out the sweet fumes of pipe tobacco. Now I pressed his pouch to my nose.

The Sheriff supervised the crew of inmates who emptied our apartment that afternoon. They lifted the oak table top off the claw-footed pedestal, carried my bed downstairs and into the truck. Groaning, they managed to get the upright piano down the steps and then pushed it across the lawn, leaving gouges in the grass. Everything would be stored in the old stable behind Grace McKee's. Years later I would hire a mover to bring it all to me at Clear Spring.

The rooms were almost empty when I saw my mother's clock. It sat silent on the mantelpiece. Winding it, keeping the steady ticking and soft chime alive, had been my father's weekly ritual.

"Do you want me to carry that?" asked Neal. We would walk back to Grace's, following the truck.

"I don't know how to wind it," I said. "How to make it ring the right time."

"Let's take it to Mr. Bolger's," he said, slipping the key into his pocket. "He'll show us how."

But I stood in the empty parlor, reluctant to leave. It was empty and strange, just a shell, but still mine for a little longer. The new jailer and his family would move in later that day.

"Come on, Hazel, let's go to get this clock going," said Neal gently. "Your dad would like that, I think."

We walked together down Juliana Street. He carried my clock in his arms, tenderly, to the jeweler's shop.

Rob Bolger, his eyes magnified by thick spectacles, his jeweler's eyepiece clamped to the glasses' frame like a tiny telescope, showed us how to wind the clock. He gently tapped the hour hand and then the minute hand around the face of the clock, chiming through each hour and half hour until he had set the time.

"Clocks don't like to be moved," he said, closing the glass face, handing me the key and the small brass pendulum from inside the back of the clock. "You may have to set the time again when you get home."

But I wasn't going home. Clocks and people don't like to be moved.

"Could we see that?" Neal asked, pointing into the glass cabinet where a ring glistened on a red plush pillow.

Mr. Bolger opened the case and drew it out. The stone was milky, but shot through with pale iridescent veins, glinting almost red. "It's a fire opal," he said.

"Do you like it?" Neal asked me.

I looked at him, not the ring, and it was like looking into a linked future, like looking into a dressing room mirror where the reflections extend and multiply. You see yourself differently, as you will be.

"Yes," I said. "It's like—like a hummingbird's throat."

"Opals are not traditional for engagements," said Mr. Bolger, cautiously, "if, excuse me, that's the occasion." Later, years later, I would learn some think opals are bad luck. I don't blame the stone, and still find it lovely, though I don't wear it often.

We had not spoken of marriage.

"Yes, we're engaged," said Neal, "or—at least I hope so."

I held out my hand and Neal slipped the ring on my finger—the ring finger on my left hand. It jammed just slightly, at the second knuckle, but fit. Fit perfectly.

"I won't even have to size that for you," said Mr. Bolger.

It cost a fortune: one hundred and thirty-five dollars.

"That's too much," I said, but Neal pulled out a fold of bills.

"What else am I going to do with this?" he said. "Over there?"

I felt a chill then, but it faded, as we walked back to Grace's, the clock in his gentle arms, the ring winking like a beacon on my finger.

We rushed headlong into marrying; not unusual, in those days. Mr. Bolger sized my parents' rose gold wedding bands, at no charge. We were both of age, and my father's friend, the Judge, exercised his wartime prerogative, waiving the three-day waiting period for a license.

"You're sure about this, Hazel?" Grace asked me.

"Yes."

"What about Bryn Mawr?"

"I'd rather wait. We'll both go to Penn State—after he's back."

For the afternoon ceremony in the upstairs chamber of the Courthouse I wore the white pique graduation dress Grace had made, and carried zinnias from her garden. Neal's best friend Joe, Neal's father, and Grace were our only guests and witnesses. She hosted our wedding supper: ham, new potatoes and peas, and an angel food cake made possible by the neighbors' pooled, generous gifts of rationed sugar. Joe brought dandelion wine from his family's cellar.

The sun, through long curtains in the dining room, cast lacey shadows on the walls as Grace lifted a crystal goblet of the pale amber wine. "To Hazel, and Neal, and absent friends." Her voice caught.

Neal's father drank too much, and fell asleep on the porch swing afterward. Joe helped him down the steps and drove him home.

Grace had given me a small leather valise, a "going away bag," though I wasn't going far. Neal and I drove away, Grace waving from the porch. We drove out of town and along Route 31, beside the Juniata River. Joe had loaned us his fishing camp for our honeymoon. A shower of insects danced in the headlights and spattered our windshield like confetti as we bounced down the rutted dirt track to the cabin.

Fireflies floated like sparks above the black cloud of foliage beside the riverbank. I smelled honeysuckle, and the vegetal green fragrance of river water, and Neal's faint sweatiness. We leaned against each other. He brushed his hand across my face, tracing my lips, and then down my neck. He slipped his long, gentle fingers into the square neckline of my dress and touched my breasts.

He carried me into the musty cabin.

"Here's the honeymoon suite," he whispered. "I'll take you to the Springs when I'm back."

The cabin had a home-made bunk bed, double berths above and below—for hunting and fishing parties. We sat on the edge of the bed for a moment—shy. And then we kissed, and lay down in the darkness, and for the next two days, and nights, we lived in the intense present moment of our bodies. We bathed in the river very early and very late—observed by no one except a solemn heron. We paddled Joe's canoe to the bend in the river where a natural dam of rocks created a swimming hole and beached the boat, wedging it into a table of tree roots. We swam in the cold, sparkling water, diving underneath to search for the fabled underwater caves. We sunned like lizards on the warm boulder. Neal showed me how to cast a line, and we cooked fish over the fire.

And then it was over: the honeymoon, and Neal's leave. Joe drove us to the Cumberland station. "Look after her," Neal said to Joe. And my husband looked at me, almost squinting with intensity.

I ran along the platform, chasing the train as it whistled its end-of-the-world blast and took Neal away.

In the long weeks that followed, only my morning shift at the Coffee Pot gave some structure to the day. I poured coffee and cut wedges of pie—strawberry rhubarb gave way to blueberry, then blackberry, then apple, then pumpkin as summer passed and gave way to fall. On rare afternoons, there would be a letter from him waiting on the marble-topped table in Grace's hallway—brief, circumspect, censored. I wrote to Neal every Sunday, spinning a filament of connection, making news out of quiet routine. I changed the time on my mother's clock; trying to approximate the time halfway across the world, in Neal's mysterious new time zone, somewhere beyond Hawaii.

The telegram arrived on Halloween, from the War Department. The doorbell rang as we ate breakfast in her bright kitchen, light streaming in through the window above the sink. After I had read it, I passed it across the table to Grace.

Missing in Action. I spun the globe in her parlor and found the sprinkle of dots representing the islands; opened the atlas and studied the page with a magnifying glass as though I would be able to see him, a speck crawling on an island beach or floating in the inlet on the map, floating in the Leyte Gulf. I marked the page with the red satin ribbon bound into the volume, and closed it.

I went back to the kitchen and scoured the clean sink with Bon Ami cleanser, running the tap full blast. I let the faucet weep the tears I could not. Grace snapped off the radio that evening, as the news proclaimed the Battle for Leyte Gulf the greatest naval battle ever fought, a triumph over the Japanese. The next morning, the old men in the Coffee Pot dropped their voices when I came to re-fill their cups, but once I was back behind the counter, they continued talking. About the battle. About the Japs. I left *The Gazette* hanging on the rack by the door, unread.

Joe came that Sunday, and every Sunday afterward, and took me to Meeting though he was not a Quaker. Looking after me, as he had promised.

Just before Thanksgiving, when I came in from work, I found an envelope addressed in Neal's graceful cursive. He'd learned his lessons well in the Common School. My hand trembled as I slit it open with the letter opener, and Grace stood beside me. For just a fraction of a moment, I dared believe he was found, recovered.

The letter was months old. Written before he even went overseas, before he was lost.

That night, my sleeping self felt the warm, heavy sweetness of Neal beside me. I awoke alone, in the bed in Grace's spare room. She heard me crying and brought me hot milk, laced with brandy.

We grieved together that year, for the double loss of my father, and of Neal. Grace taught her students, and played Chopin etudes to herself, late into the night.

I forced myself to write to Neal, care of the Red Cross. It felt necessary, as though writing to him was somehow a charm to keep him alive, an attempt to convince myself I still believed.

Grace suggested I enroll at Bryn Mawr, for the second semester.

"No. I'll transfer to Penn State—later. After."

If I left, if I started my life without him, that would be giving up.

I sleep-walked through the winter and the spring. Sleep-walked into summer, the anniversaries of my father's death, my wedding. Waiting. Waiting. Waiting.

Waiting, my father and the Quakers would say, for the Way to open. Waiting to discern what I was meant to do next. But for me it was nothing so active, as purposeful as that. It was limbo. It was treading water.

But in the summer, that summer of 1945, the Way did open.

Or rather, the Bedford Springs re-opened. The hotel had been closed since January when the last student of the Keystone Naval Training School graduated. But now they were looking for personnel. And guards!

The gossip spread like wildfire through town that warm morning in July. I heard it first among my customers, the weathered old men who spent hours at the Coffee Pot.

"Dollars to donuts, it's going to be a POW camp—like Emmitsburg."

"Why would they put the lousy Krauts in such a fancy place? They're in a Conservation Corps Camp over in Emmitsburg."

"Don't know, but I'm going to this meeting the State Department's holding there. To find out."

In spite of myself, I felt a quickening of interest. Something was happening.

Joe called that afternoon. "Have you heard about the meeting over at the Springs? Want to come?"

Cars lined both sides of the driveway, filled the lot beside the golf course, and parked all along the bank above Shober's Run across from the hotel. The main building blazed with light, as though for a pre-war party. But the wear and tear of three years as a military training school showed. The lawn was ragged, and the floors inside were scuffed.

Joe gripped the banister as we climbed the staircase to the ballroom. His narrow jaw was clenched. Usually I forgot his bad leg. He was a small man, compact and strong and never one to complain. But these stairs required effort.

"Look—the walkway door," he said. The hotel had an elevated footbridge leading across the lawn and road to the paths on the hillside where Neal and I had played as children. Now the door from the landing to the footbridge was chained shut.

"They really are going to have prisoners here," I said, feeling again the flutter of excitement. It was like waking up. Something important was happening here! The war was coming here. Finally, there would be real events to report in my next letter to Neal—or the idea of Neal I tried to hold onto.

The ballroom was packed. We took seats in the very last row of folding chairs. I recognized neighbors, customers, the Clerk of the Friends Meeting, and classmates from school. My father's old friend the Sheriff was seated up front on the stage with the Mayor—alongside strangers in uniform and dark suits. And many in the crowd were strangers, too.

"Who are all these people?" I whispered to Joe.

"People from D.C., from all over," he said. "This is putting Bedford on the map." He was right. The next week there would even be a story about Bedford in *Newsweek* magazine. The meeting had drawn people from Cumberland, Johnstown, Altoona and Pittsburgh; VFW chapters and Gold Star Mothers from all over western Pennsylvania; and State Department and military officials from Washington.

The Mayor stood at the podium, which was emblazoned on the front in gold script with *The Bedford Springs Hotel.*

"Good evening. Let me introduce John E. Peurifoy, from the State Department."

A tall, distinguished looking man with gray hair, wearing a light gray suit, took the podium. There was something fancy about the suit, different. I was sorry Grace hadn't come. "Thank you all for being here. Let me introduce my colleagues Albert Clattenburg and Robert Bannerman." Two men seated on the stage rose and nodded. Mr. Peurifoy continued, "And we are most fortunate to have here tonight two leaders of two very important organizations. Pennsylvania State Commander of the American Legion, William Rhodes. And Edward Linsky, State Adjutant of the Veterans of Foreign Wars. We appreciate their generosity in joining us here to address the needs and interests of the people of Pennsylvania as we prepare the Bedford Springs Hotel for the internment of the Japanese Ambassador to Germany and others captured with him when Berlin fell to our forces in May."

There was a buzzing in the crowd as though a volt of electricity had just shot through the room. "Japs!" shouted a shrill voice from the crowd. "I say burn the Springs down before we let filthy Japs stay here!"

Heckling and catcalls broke out. The Sheriff stood, and I suddenly noticed his deputies—some of them men I knew from my father's poker games—step forward from around the room. I missed my father's calm and steadiness, and leaned closer to Joe. There was an ugly feeling in the air.

The deputies escorted the man who had started the heckling outside. The muttering subsided.

Mr. Peurifoy tapped on the microphone. "I must stress these detainees are of course our enemy, but not military combatants, not ordinary prisoners. Ambassador Hiroshi Oshima and his staff and their families are valuable bargaining collateral, blue chips certain to secure the release of some of our 14,000 servicemen held by the Japanese."

Like Neal, I thought, if he's alive. He's alive! I admonished myself.

"Like Neal," whispered Joe to me. If he had any doubt, he never showed it. All I could see was hope and certainty alight in his gray eyes. I wished it was so simple for me.

Mr. Peurifoy continued. "These detainees are diplomats. They pose no danger to your community. They are of utmost value.'

"Our boys aren't eating bonbons in luxury hotels!" shouted a hoarse voice. A chorus of grumbling agreement swept the crowd.

"I appreciate that," said Mr. Peurifoy, shouting to be heard. "But this hotel has been selected for its secure location—your lovely valley is narrow and isolated—an excellent, natural setting for secure detention. Needless to say, the detainees will have no access to the recreation facilities. They will be held here in strict accordance with the Geneva Convention, treated fairly, but without luxuries."

"Our boys in Bataan didn't get fair! They got tortured! Put these Japs in a prison in D.C.! Don't send garbage here!"

The deputies removed several hecklers. Mr. Peurifoy went on, seemingly unperturbed.

"Hotels are actually the most efficient and economical internment sites. I have charts on display in the lobby to illustrate how we will use the hotel's buildings. A seven-foot fence is being erected on the road. Floodlights installed. The National Guard will provide security."

Someone called out. "How will you feed these people? Out of our rations?"

The Sheriff and two deputies walked up and down the center aisle. The protest died down.

"The government will pay full price. Most of the food will come from out of town. And there will be opportunities for employment here for you."

"You couldn't pay me enough to work with the filthy Japs," someone behind me hissed.

Mr. Peurifoy stepped away from the podium. "And now, it is a great honor to present Brigadier General Leonard Boyd, just back from the Pacific Theater," he said.

A gaunt, tan man in a beribboned uniform stepped to the podium.

Cheering, waving, and clapping, the audience stood.

The General nodded and spoke. He had a fierce expression, and a loud voice.

"Good evening. I am here to tell you tonight you have the honor to be part of an important effort. A month ago, I was with our men in the Pacific theater. Thanks to the efforts of our men—your men—

we have the enemy on the run. They're getting what they deserve, and I'm going back to finish the job."

Shouts and a thunder of feet stomping erupted. I glanced at Joe. His pale skin was flushed.

"Your community has a job to do. I request complete cooperation with the State Department. These prisoners are the key for the door to exchange. The Japs will give up your boys and our own General Jonathan Wainwright, hero of Corregidor, to get Ambassador Oshima back." Pandemonium broke out: cheers and stamping.

Joe pumped his fist into the air. "I'm going to work here!" he shouted.

"Me too!" I yelled. "Me too!"

Chapter Two

Oppressive, ominous heat shimmered in the evening air, as though even the mountains held their breath in the suspense of waiting for the Japanese prisoners to arrive. I'd sweated through my starched white blouse, turning the stiff fabric limp over the long day of final preparation.

Approaching traffic boomed beyond the pine stockade fence. The border patrols, pistols bulging on hips, straightened beside the new sentry box, and opened the gate. A caravan of buses from Cumberland—emblazoned *Queen City Blue and Gold*—roared up the drive and ground to a halt in front of the hotel. The windows were blackened: whoever waited inside couldn't see out.

I shivered with suspense.

"This is it," said Joe. He radiated excitement, though he'd been disappointed—relegated to maintenance rather than guard work, again deprived of a gun and military uniform.

My own assignment had proved better than I could have dreamed. Thanks to my typing speed and shorthand (acquired in the high school business course), I won the practice drills for the job of personal secretary to the State Department's representative, the man in charge: Lytton Phelps.

"So you're a Quaker?" Mr. Phelps had asked the first morning I reported to his office.

"Yes." Would it be held against me?

"Does the name Terasaki Hidenari mean anything to you?"

"No, sir."

"First Secretary to the Japanese Embassy in Washington when Pearl Harbor occurred," he said. "I knew him. He married an American Quaker. He and she, and their daughter, are in Japan now—sent in a prisoner swap, actually, like what we'll be doing here, on a much larger scale."

"I never heard of him."

"There've been plenty of Quakers in Japan—Emperor Hirohito's mother Sadako was raised by Japanese Quakers, taught by them in the Peeress's school. I must be certain you hold no sympathies that would interfere."

"My husband is missing in action in the Pacific. I want to do whatever I can."

"I see," he said, regarding me over his spectacles. Neal's status clinched it.

My selection for the position aroused envy; as though I'd been singled out as teacher's pet. That morning, killing time, waiting for the detainees to arrive, the other girls assembled for a group photo beneath the flag pole. I passed by, trying to look nonchalant. Cora, a former classmate, called out. "Come be in the picture, Hazel!"

Cora—smelling of soap suds and furniture polish—put her arm around my waist. In the picture, I look out of place among the smiling girls linked arm to waist. The sturdy paper dolls wear white uniforms and frilled aprons. My straight skirt and tailored blouse (Grace's gift, from her own clothing ration) and serious expression set me apart.

"Here they come!" said Joe. "Here they come!"

The door of the first bus opened; the driver emerged and placed a foot stool on the ground. A Japanese man—short, but broad and imposing—appeared, flourishing a cane with a silver head. He wore a bold, challenging expression—like a boxer in the ring.

"That's him. The top diplo-rat, Ambassador Hiroshi Oshima," said Joe.

Several men in dark suits and elegant homburg hats, carrying leather brief cases, followed the Ambassador across the lawn to Lytton Phelps.

Although my boss towered over the Ambassador, the smaller man looked commanding. Mr. Phelps extended his hand; the Ambassador ignored it and bowed instead, with an obsequious arrogance.

"I'd spit in his eye," said Joe, despite the pledge the State Department required that we treat the "visitors" with respect.

"Acts as though he's doing us a favor, being here," said Prudence Johnson, the stout middle-aged woman in charge of the kitchen. She'd worked at the hotel for years, had stayed on during the Navy's sojourn, and was still complaining about their rough treatment of "her" hotel. One by one, Japanese men emerged from the first buses; most dressed in fine tailored suits, though a few younger men wore more casual clothes.

"Look at all the glasses," said Mrs. Johnson. "Japs have weak eyes."

I didn't point out that Prudence Johnson herself wore spectacles.

The first woman appeared: diminutive, gray-haired, wearing a navy blue dress with white cuffs and collar, a dark straw hat, white gloves. A younger woman, carrying a violin case and an umbrella, came next. They stood on the lawn; the young woman put down her violin and opened the umbrella, holding it above the older woman as a sunshade.

"Mrs. Ambassador and her maid," said Mrs. Johnson. "Careful of her yellow skin."

The skin, actually, was very pale, almost translucent.

Next came more women, and children. A little boy stumbled, landing with bare knees on gravel. His slender mother knelt and brushed him off. He crouched on the lawn, plucking blades of grass, tossing them up, and showering himself. A gangly young girl ran up and down, flapping her hands, head twitching.

"Retarded," sniffed Mrs. Johnson. "They're inbred."

Her mother caught the girl in a tight embrace, pinning down her aimless arms. The girl's agitated movements subsided but she whined like a frightened animal. The other children pulled away from her, solemn and still, clutching stuffed toys, wearing rucksacks.

Joe exhaled a very soft wolf whistle. "Look at that!"

A woman, taller than any of the Japanese women or men, stood on the steps of the bus.

Sunlight glinted on a fringe of copper curls beneath a navy blue straw hat. A fine mesh veil hid her eyes; a green purse dangled from her arm. She smoothed her straight skirt over shapely hips with white-gloved hands.

One of the local girls, hired for kitchen help, hissed under her breath. "Must be a kraut married to a Jap."

A girl with auburn hair, about twelve or thirteen years old, stood beside the woman before hurrying across the lawn to a slender man wearing a charcoal gray suit. He was very handsome; a shock of black hair swept back from a broad forehead.

"They have a kid," one of the girls said. "Look at that. A mongrel kid."

And that was my introduction to Charlotte, her mother, and her father.

Phelps escorted the Ambassador and his wife up the stairs.

"Welcome to Bedford Springs," he said, holding open the door to the lobby.

The guards herded the detainees into a long line for processing.

The prisoners would be housed in the attached frame wings telescoping out of the main building. Every guest room in the hotel opened off a long balcony running the length of the structure, designed to catch the breezes.

Like the rest of the women on the staff, I had a small maid's room in the fourth floor attic above the guests' rooms. Phelps's lodgings and office were behind the hotel, in the manager's residence, the Cottage. The maintenance staff and the guards bunked in the Annex, a dormitory built into the steep slope behind the hotel. That hillside formed a natural wall; its location and geology made the hotel ideal for the State Department's purpose. According to the contract I'd filed, the State Department was authorized to use the main brick building as well as the residential wings at a rate of $3.50 a day for each "guest." The owner also was receiving $1.50 a day for each staff member and "necessary government personnel." An extra ten percent had been assessed to cover "the depreciation of china, glassware, linens, management overhead, depreciation of fixed equipment, and wear and tear on the building." It seemed like an awful lot of money!

My boss had delegated me to help with registration. I perched on a high stool behind the massive oak lobby desk next to Ada, the switchboard operator. Older (at least twenty-five), glamorous and flirtatious in her tight skirt and red lipstick, she intimidated me. Now she tapped her manicured fingers impatiently on the chart of room assignments.

We checked off the Oshimas on the State Department manifest. Next, the Ambassador's valet presented his papers, followed by the young woman with the violin—*Suwa, Nejiko, Miss, 25, Private*

Secretary to Mrs. Oshima.

Joe saluted Phelps and triumphantly took charge of escorting the Ambassador's party to their rooms. Despite his limp, Joe marched up the stairs as though finally going into battle. Oshima followed, brandishing his cane, letting his valet struggle with two suitcases and a briefcase.

Until that day, I'd never seen an Oriental person—we didn't even have a Chinese restaurant or laundry in Bedford. There were more than a hundred detainees, more Japanese than us! I tried not to gawk as one by one, family by family, we registered the visitors, collected their passports and immigration documents. I found each name on my list, wondering how I would remember who was who, how I would ever tell them apart.

Assada, Eiji, Embassy Clerk, 39.

Assada, Mitsuko, Wife, 35.

Assada, Kimi, Daughter, 5.

Doi, Tatsu, Physician, 50.

A doctor, I thought. A Japanese doctor!

Fukuzawa, Shintaro, Special Attaché, 33.

Fukuzawa, Sashiko, Wife, 29.

Fukuzawa, Kiyoko, Daughter, 1.

Mrs. Fukuzawa, a plump woman with a worried expression, held her daughter. The little girl looked at me, round and perfect as one of Grace's Japanese dolls.

I smiled at the child; the little girl shut her eyes and burrowed into her mother.

Igarasi, Hiroshi, Chancellor, 45.

Igarasi, Hide, Wife, 35.

Igarasi, Chizuko, Daughter, 4.

Igarasi, Isamu, Son, 6.

Kagata, Chiyoko, Maid, 27.

Ono, Shichiro, Journalist, 37.

Ono, Momoyo, Wife, 35.

Ono, Mitsuharu, Son, 11.

Goto, Shigeru, Military Attaché's Servant, 32.

Hibiki, Fumiko, Attendant, 26.

Hori, Hisayoshi, Embassy Clerk, 56.

Kawarada, Keishi, Attaché, 27.

Takano, Toshi, Chef, 55.

Inoue, Tadashi, Attaché, 35.

Inoue, Yoshiko, Wife, 37.

Inoue, Minoru, Son, 8.

The mixed couple approached. At close range, I noticed again how very handsome he was. This man stood out—his face looked almost like a sculpture. Quite a few spoke at least some English, but with accents I found hard to understand. His was perfect.

"We're the Harada family," he said.

I ran my finger down the roster:

Harada, Takeo, Special Attaché, 37.

Harada, Gwendolyn, Wife, 35.

Harada, Charlotte, Daughter, 13.

"I need to speak to whoever is in charge," said his wife. Her accent was English—like in the movies. She wasn't German after all! "There's been a serious error. I'm British. My daughter and I should not be prisoners here. I need to speak to someone in charge," she repeated, louder, as though she'd not been heard the first time. "We must be sent home directly." Anxious green eyes peered out from behind the veil on her hat. She looked tired, on the verge of coming apart. Even her brooch, a gold feather, dangled askew.

"I demand to speak to your supervisor." Her voice trembled.

"Gwendolyn," said her husband, placing their documents on the desk.

Their daughter bit her lip, looking anxiously back and forth between her parents.

"I demand to speak to the man in charge," the woman repeated, her voice growing shrill.

"Go get Mr. Phelps," said Ada.

"What's the problem?" asked Lytton Phelps.

"She says she's English," said Ada. "Wants special handling."

"I *am* British. Sir, please contact the ambassador."

"Madam, the Ambassador has been taken to his room. It has already been a very long day. I will speak with Mr. Oshima about your situation in due course."

"I mean *my* ambassador, the British Ambassador in Washington D.C. I must see you, privately."

"I will be glad to see you by appointment, but not today," said Mr. Phelps, in a calm, measured tone despite an angry glint in his pale blue eyes. "Joe, please show the Haradas to their room."

"Sharing a room with him is out of the question," said the woman, gesturing to her husband. Her husband gazed at a point in midair, as though removing himself from the scene. The girl looked close to tears.

"Mrs. Harada," said Mr. Phelps. "I have no provisions for arranging separate accommodations at this time. I will speak with Ambassador Oshima, and the Secretary. Nothing can be changed without going through channels, certainly not today."

Fuming, she followed Joe out of the lobby.

"What a drama," said Ada, smiling as though she'd enjoyed it. I felt profoundly uncomfortable. The steady stream of prisoners continued, distracting me:

Matsui, Sashichiro, Attaché, 32.

Otani, Kotaro, First Secretary. 42.

Suddenly, the odd girl Mrs. Johnson had called retarded broke to the head of the line, whining, flapping her hands. A guard grabbed her, and the girl lunged, trying to bite him. Her mother arrived. "Forgive me, I'm so sorry," the woman said to the guard, slowly and clearly, in English. The girl broke away and hid behind her mother.

Mitsuno, Keiko, 44, Widow of Naval Attaché Toyu Mitsuno.

Mitsuno, Mia, Daughter, 11.

The woman handed me her documents. "My husband was in charge of the Japanese Embassy in Italy. He was killed last year by Italian partisans and we came to Berlin to be under Ambassador Oshima's protection. Please excuse my daughter. She—she's not well."

"She's a nut case is what she is," said Ada after the woman and girl had left.

Finally, every internee had been registered and shown upstairs; the documents locked away.

"Anything else for me now, sir?" I asked Mr. Phelps.

"Not at present, Hazel," he said. "I may need you later though."

Ada fanned herself. "So we've got marital troubles and mental defectives, good Lord," she said, gloating. The phone rang and she swiveled to the switchboard. "Bedford Springs," she answered in her lilting voice.

I slipped out from behind the reception desk and walked through the lobby. Something gold glittered on the floor by the door—the red-haired English woman's pretty feather brooch. I have always hated losing things, and felt a pang of sympathy for Mrs. Gwendolyn Harada with her strange combined name, and marriage, and daughter. I would return the pin to her. Putting the brooch in my pocket, I wandered outside and along the porch. The new fence obscured the view of the golf links and the mountains beyond. Ordinarily, it would be the kind of evening made for a long walk or playing croquet in the deepening dusk. Sitting in a rocking chair, I listened to footsteps and the subdued murmur of voices from the balconies above. The hotel had guests again. The detainees were settling in.

***

The brass gong in the lobby sang out, announcing supper. The Japanese filed down the stairs, along the porch, and through the lobby to the dining room. A line of tables placed end to end beside the swinging kitchen doors served as the buffet. Tonight, Mrs. Johnson herself presided over a light meal of sandwiches and soup. Meals would be cafeteria style. Mrs. Johnson complained the higher-ups in D.C. had no clue as to how hard it would be to provide meals on her budget, within rationing. "Whether you've got sit-down service or an assembly line, food costs the same." She'd spoken to Mr. Phelps already about the quality and quantity of her fresh supplies as well as the meager first shipment of supplemental canned goods from the commissary in D.C. "The miracle of the loaves and fishes will look easy compared to feeding almost two hundred on this." Despite her grumbling, she seemed grimly delighted by the challenge of making do and proud of proving her culinary ingenuity by substituting grain for meat. She'd already had me type up several days' menus: Cottage Cheese Fondue, Vegetable and Oatmeal Goulash, Sausage Cornuts.

Ambassador Oshima and his wife led the line into the dining room. He chose a table by the long French windows beside the porch, and sent two attendants back through the buffet line to bring the couple their food.

The rest of the detainees bowed as they accepted their meal, murmuring *a-ri-ga-to-o, thank you, thank you.*

Takeo Harada arrived alone, and sat alone. His wife and daughter arrived later, but did not join him. Mrs. Harada had dressed for dinner, and rustled past in a wrinkled black taffeta dress. Her red hair was gathered into a sleek bun, showing off a strand of pearls around a long, slender neck. The girl seemed uncomfortable, reluctantly following the woman across the room to sit at a table in the corner farthest from Mr. Harada.

Last of all came the widow Mrs. Mitsuno and her unfortunate daughter; the girl gobbled down her food, rocking back and forth.

"Poor little thing," said Cora. "Hazel, Mrs. Johnson sent me over to tell you to eat now, if you want to fill a plate. We'll be cleaning up soon."

Lytton Phelps made a brief speech after dinner, pausing every few sentences while a woman detainee translated. The Japanese was completely incomprehensible. I had never met anyone before whose first language was a foreign language, and never heard anything like this rapid cascade of syllables. How amazing that these people understood what she was saying!

"Welcome to Bedford Springs. I have reported your arrival to the Secretary of State. Rest assured, all provisions of Geneva will be honored. Be advised, there is to be no use of any of the recreational facilities by detainees. Remain in the main buildings and on the main grounds. The other areas are cordoned off and entry is strictly forbidden. Evening curfew will be ten p.m. There is to be no attempt to send uncensored external communication of any sort to anyone. All written communications must be in English, and turned in at the desk. After review a determination will be made on a case by case basis regarding forwarding any of your correspondence. Now, on behalf of my government, I again extend our welcome and our hope that your stay here will be brief and productive. We look forward to returning you to Japan at the earliest possible time, providing your Government proves cooperative."

Ambassador Oshima bowed, both courteous and haughty at once.

After dinner, most of the men walked circular laps around the front lawn while the women sat on the porch in the long row of rockers, talking softly. I lingered at the end of the porch. On the side lawn, the children played tag and chased fireflies with delighted shrieks. An elderly Japanese man, small, wearing a beret, shuffled up beside me. He bowed.

"Good evening, Mademoiselle. Takano, at your service. What a delight to see the fireflies. At home, we celebrate Firefly Night in June."

"What's that?" He seemed sweet, harmless.

"Every child has a collecting bag. The sacks glow like lanterns by the end of the hunt when the children set the fireflies free again."

Strains of music, piano and violin, wafted along the porch.

"Ah," he said. "Miss Suwa and Mrs. Harada. This will be a treat."

I followed him to the open French doors at the lounge. The English woman was at the piano and Mrs. Oshima's secretary, Nejiko Suwa, was playing the violin. A small audience, including the Ambassador's wife, Lytton Phelps, Takeo Harada and his daughter Charlotte, listened. The room had been stripped of carpets and curtains before the prisoners arrived; the music echoed in the bare room. I slipped into the room and leaned against one of the bookcases I had emptied earlier in the week, packing the books away in boxes for the duration, like the hotel china.

Once, Grace McKee had taken me to Pittsburgh for a concert. But I had never heard a piano sound so rich, a violin so sad. I wished Grace McKee could hear this. She would know the composer; I thought I recognized Brahms. When Nejiko Suwa lowered her bow, when the English woman lifted her fingers from the keyboard, the small assembly broke into applause. The two women smiled, nodded, and continued to play on, holding us spellbound. Nejiko Suwa seemed to sink into another space, holding her violin so tenderly, her eyes on the music. And I couldn't help but watch the way Takeo Harada looked across the room at his wife. I wanted someone to look at me that way again. The way Neal had.

The curfew siren split the air. Odd little Mia burst into the room, shrieking, pounding her fingers on her head. Takeo Harada corralled the child until her mother arrived. "I am so sorry," the woman said, bowing. "The siren frightened her." Mrs. Mitsuno held her daughter by the shoulders, saying something to her that calmed her. The girl dropped a quick, jerky bow to Mr. Harada. Mrs. Mitsuno walked her daughter away, held close to her side. Under her wing, like a mother bird, I thought.

Gwendolyn Harada closed the keyboard and picked up a sheaf of music.

I lingered, and heard her murmur to the violinist, "The first decent piano I've touched since leaving Berlin. Better tuned than that one in Bad Gastein." So that was how you pronounced it, I thought. Bad Gastein. The prisoners had been captured in Austria, trying to reach Switzerland after Berlin fell. The files I had read as I put them away said that our Japanese diplomats had been held in another resort hotel, in the mountains of Austria, before coming here. What strange prisoners; what strange prisons. I wished I could tell my father.

After everyone left, I sat at the piano and picked out *Somewhere Over the Rainbow*. The song seemed like a memory of another life. Had only six years passed since I'd sat in the Pitt Theatre, in darkness fragrant with spilled soda and stale popcorn?

"Sounds nice," said Joe. When had he come in?

"Did you hear the women playing? It was—better than when Grace McKee took me to Pittsburgh."

"I'm not much for the classical stuff," he said, leaning on the piano. In work clothes, he looked out of place against the glossy wood of the Steinway. Pale and slight, quiet—in primary school he'd always been one of the last called to join teams in the playground relays, but he had a fine voice. The teacher said he had perfect pitch and always had him sing a solo in the Christmas concert. I thought he might sing now, but he didn't.

I stopped playing, embarrassed.

"Ping pong?" he asked.

Lytton Phelps said staff could continue to use the recreation facilities when not on duty, providing we left the rooms secured and practiced "utmost discretion." I'd taken advantage of his permission during the hectic week of preparation to swim in the indoor pool in the recreation wing—Mrs. Johnson boasted it was the first and best in the country. Joe and I had played ping pong several times while guards shot pool on the tables left behind by the Navy radio school.

Tonight, no one else was in the game room when Joe unlocked the door and flicked on the light switch. The cavernous room held two ping pong tables, two pool tables, and a left behind washtub base from the Mountain Navy. Even in summer, the air smelled of wood smoke from a winter's worth of blazes in the massive fieldstone fireplace.

"Your serve," said Joe, stepping to the table, picking up a paddle and tossing the ball over the net to me. We volleyed back and forth, the rhythmic click of ball and thunk of paddles substituting for conversation.

After our game, I rocked by the empty fire place. Joe pulled a pack of Camels out of his shirt pocket. My father didn't drink, but he smoked one cigarette every evening after dinner, reading in his chair, and enjoyed a pipe on his card nights. Neal smoked, too. On our brief honeymoon, I awoke alone and found him sitting by the embers of the fire outside, his cigarette tip glowing in the darkness. I tried Neal's cigarette, but it made me cough. Now the scent of smoke comforted me, and made me ache with loneliness.

We walked back toward the main building, separating at the path to Joe's quarters in the Annex. I continued alone along the dark porch. Lytton Phelps had forbidden us to use the interior hallways which connected the rambling wings of the hotel. The elevator was likewise off limits. He ordered, for security purposes, that everyone— prisoners and staff alike—remain visible at all times, going up and down the porch and exterior stairs, to and fro on the long balconies outside the bedrooms.

"Who's that?" called a rough voice.

"It's me, Hazel," I said.

"Identify yourself, if you're prowling around alone at night," cautioned the guard.

I climbed up, passing the second and third floor landings—the floors where the detainees were housed and would be already asleep. Opening the door to my room beneath the eaves, the stored heat of the day hit me like warmth from an oven. On the bureau, Neal's face, square-jawed and resolute, stared out at me from the picture frame; the tick of my mother's clock measured the solitude. I had let the chimes run down though, not wanting to disturb the other girls. And I had set it to our time. I could no longer even pretend to imagine Neal going through a day in some distant Pacific time-zone.

Unbuttoning my blouse, folding my skirt, I discovered Gwendolyn Harada's gold feather brooch, forgotten in my pocket. Return it tomorrow, I reminded myself, pulling on my cotton batiste nightgown, crawling into bed.

Overtired, I tossed on the warm sheets, flipping my pillow to the cooler side. Images of the day crowded the darkness: arrogant Oshima, solemn children, Takeo Harada's dark eyes staring at his wife across the room.

I gave up on sleeping. I needed air, and descended the steep stairs from the attic rooms to the third floor balcony below. Leaning against the balustrade, I looked out into rustling leaves and listened to the water in Shober's Run beyond the fence.

A white figure flitted across the lawn, illuminated by the light streaming from the sentry box.

"Who's there?" called a guard.

The ghost darted between the trees.

"Halt!"

"Mia, Mia!" A woman's voice called out; another shadowy figure ran through the beam of the searchlight.

A guard waved a flashlight across the lawn, illuminating the girl and her mother.

"Keep her inside!" the guard ordered. Mrs. Mitsuno led her wailing daughter back to the building, chiding her with an incomprehensible cascade of sounds.

Early the next morning, before five, even before the first birds, I awoke. This had been my swimming time. But I felt uneasy—aware of the invisible presence of the prisoners sleeping in their rooms below. Before, the empty hotel had seemed like my private world. Every morning I had watched the sky redden as I walked along the quiet veranda to the pool. Now I hesitated, inhibited. If I listened hard enough, I could almost hear them breathing, snoring, sleeping.

You're not a prisoner, I reminded myself. Go! Before anyone is up!

Morning mist rose off the grass below as I hurried down the staircase along the porch to the lobby. The guard on night watch at the reception desk looked up from his solitaire game and slid the key to the pool across the counter.

"You're the early bird," he said. "You must love the water. Too cold for me this time of day. Though I wouldn't say no to a dip in the lake across the way, one afternoon." He was from away, one of the border patrols Mr. Phelps had imported. Was it my imagination, or was he flirting with me? I took the key clumsily, retrieving it with my left hand to make sure he saw my rings.

I unlocked the door, climbed the staircase, and slipped into one of the curtained alcoves off the gallery to change.

Diving in, I swam a length underwater and then my laps. Afterward, I floated on my back, gazing at the blue ceiling above me. Swimming here, the room illuminated by light from the clerestory, swimming in mineral water, was almost like swimming in an open air pavilion.

I felt someone watching, and stopped to tread water. It was the odd girl, Mia, peering from behind a column. How had she followed me? Mr. Phelps would put an end to swimming if he learned about this. Clambering out of the pool, grabbing my robe, I chased her along the slippery tile deck and dragged her by her skinny arm to the lobby.

"I'm sorry," I said, over her shrieks. "But you can't come here." Of course she didn't understand and just yelled louder.

Her mother ran toward us. So quickly I almost didn't believe my eyes, Mrs. Mitsuno slapped her daughter once on the cheek. The girl's cries subsided instantly. Her mother bowed to me and then hurried her daughter upstairs.

"I didn't see that kid go by," said the guard. "She's a handful. How was your dip?"

"Fine," I said, returning the key. From his sly smile, I knew he wouldn't tell anyone what happened. Phelps wouldn't know.

After dressing, my hair still a little damp from my swim, I joined the other staff in the small dining room off the kitchen for breakfast.

"He wants his breakfast right away." Mrs. Johnson handed me Lytton Phelps's breakfast tray. "You'll have to eat later."

I hurried up the steep hill to the cottage. Mr. Phelps used the back parlor as his office; my own desk, filing cabinet, and typing table filled the front parlor. Pocket doors between could be closed for the illusion of privacy, though every sound remained audible, particularly when he had to shout to make himself heard on a bad telephone connection. Especially since he knew I could overhear, he stressed the importance of confidentiality. I prided myself on keeping what I learned secret, telling no one, not even Joe. With a sense of great importance, I stamped my boss's correspondence, and the documents regarding the detainees, "*Classified.*"

"Here is your breakfast, sir." Mr. Phelps looked up, took off his glasses and rubbed his eyes. He'd been at his desk already at least an hour. My boss worked long hours, and adhered to regular habits, eating the same breakfast every day of the weeks I would work for him: poached eggs and toast, black coffee.

"I'm expecting one of the internees for an appointment shortly. File these dossiers on the Embassy employees, and lock the cabinets."

I knelt by the metal cabinet beside my desk. Reading as I filed was one of the perks of my job though everything I learned must be kept secret. The amount of detail in each dossier varied. Some contained barely more than birth date, birthplace, position in the Embassy, and the individual's name—in English and Japanese characters, handwritten hieroglyphics. Others provided more background. Who would have expected a doctor of philosophy among them, who had taught at a German university? A chef who had run a Japanese restaurant in Paris? Mrs. Oshima's secretary, I learned, had been a professional violinist. And some records bore disturbing handwritten notes: "This individual does not have immunity status. A thorough interrogation was performed." And, occasionally, a further notation: "cooperative" or "un-cooperative." Somehow, I didn't like the sound of it. What exactly was a "thorough interrogation"? What happened to someone who was not cooperative?

I was particularly curious about the dossier stamped "Harada, Takeo & Family" and sat cross-legged on the floor, reading it carefully.

Birth date: 6 February, 1908. Passport Number: 340154. Special Attaché, Japanese Embassy Berlin. Date of Appointment: May, 1937. Last home address in Japan: No. 286 Chojamuru, Kami-Osaki, Shinagawa-ku, Nagasaki; date of departure August, 1926. Subsequent itinerary: Oxford University (Economics, 1926-1930), London School of Economics (1930-1931), Japanese Embassy London (1931-1937). Dependents: Gwendolyn Mason (35, m. 1931); Charlotte, (13) Daughter.

Engrossed, I did not hear Gwendolyn Harada until she stood at my desk.

"I have an appointment."

I scrambled to my feet, guiltily turning over the documents.

She wore a white blouse and a navy blue skirt, and a delicious scent. How did she manage to seem so elegant, in spite of everything? The pearls around her neck reminded me; I felt in my pocket for her gold feather brooch.

"I think this might be yours."

"Thank you," she said, gratefully, but with a faintly suspicious expression.

"I found it," I said, as though accused.

"Thank you," she said again. "It was my mother's. I hate losing anything more."

I know how that is, I might have said, but Mr. Phelps appeared in the doorway to his office. "Ah, Mrs. Harada. I so enjoyed listening to you and Mrs. Oshima's secretary. She is remarkable. And what tone her instrument has."

"Nejiko is conservatory trained. The violin is a Stradivarius."

My boss looked shocked. "No. Where did she get it?"

Mrs. Harada seemed to hesitate a moment. "A gift," she said. "From Minister Goebbels," she added, dropping her voice.

"And where did he get it?" Mr. Phelps sounded angry. What exactly was a Stradivarius? And this Minister Goebbels—I recognized his name from the papers, one of the evil ones.

"Stolen," snapped my boss. "It should have been confiscated in Le Havre, with the other contraband." I'd read the lists: swords, cameras, revolvers—golf clubs!

Mrs. Harada looked frightened now. "Please, don't take it from her. We've all lost so much," she said. And I recalled what she had said when I returned the little pin.

Mr. Phelps ushered her into his office, but did not close the pocket doors. I sat at my desk, listening.

"Thank you for meeting with me. I apologize for being so distraught yesterday, but my situation is—well, unendurable, intolerable."

"It is difficult for all of you. But given the unfortunate circumstances, that is to be expected."

"But we—my daughter and I—are in a very unique position. We cannot possibly remain here with these others."

"But Mrs. Harada, your predicament is of your own making. You are married to a member of the ambassador's staff, a Japanese national."

"Call me Gwendolyn, please. I married my husband in a different time, fourteen years ago. I never dreamed what was coming. His posting to Berlin, the war—being cut off from everything, everyone."

"Unfortunate consequences of your free decision."

"I didn't know! Now, I do. I must divorce him. I cannot go to Japan. My daughter should not be punished."

"I have no authority in this matter. It's impossible anyway," he said. "You won't be here long, and you are not a legal resident."

"At least contact my embassy. I should be considered a refugee."

"Hardly, Mrs. Harada. There is really nothing I can do."

"You could ask. And provide a separate room for myself and for Charlotte?" Her voice trembled. "It is not good for her, to hear us discussing—our predicament."

After a long pause, clearing his throat, my boss said, "I will do what I can about your accommodations, Mrs. Harada." He kept a photograph of his own daughters on his desk. People said he was divorced. The first divorced man I had ever encountered. His usually formal tone sounded almost sympathetic.

"And I will advise the British Embassy of your presence. Beyond that, there is nothing I can do."

"But for my daughter's sake—please ask my embassy to help me at least reach my parents, get some word to them. I've heard nothing from them all this time. They lived—live—in London. I must know what has happened."

"Mrs. Harada, I cannot grant you any special favors. Hazel!"

I stepped into the office. He sat behind the bulwark of his desk, forehead shining with perspiration. The woman dabbed at her eyes with a handkerchief.

"Show Mrs. Harada back to the hotel, please. And please find Miss Suwa and bring her here. With her violin."

"Please, sir," said Mrs. Harada. "I am not certain about the violin—it will break her heart if you take it away."

"Good day," he said firmly.

The woman was crying as we walked. She stumbled as we descended the steep gravel path, limping just ahead of me. The impractical shoes were scuffed, and I could see a blister on her heel. She did not seem so intimidating, so elegant, now.

We found Nejiko Suwa in her room, on the second floor, just past the room where Ambassador Oshima and his wife stayed. Her door was open and the sound of her practicing floated along the balcony. Children played by the railing under the watchful eyes of their mothers who were rocking and fluttering bright paper fans. The women had been talking softly, but fell silent as we approached.

"Nejiko," said the English woman, tapping on the door frame. The music stopped. The violinist came to the door, wrapped in a blue and white robe. A kimono, I thought.

"Ah, Gwen. Let's do the Brahms tonight." Her English had a lilt to it. A French accent perhaps? How worldly these women were. It dazzled me.

"Nejiko, forgive me, but I was speaking with Mr. Phelps. He complimented your playing, asked me about the violin." Her voice trailed away.

"You didn't tell—who gave it to me?"

Mrs. Harada looked stricken. "I'm sorry—but we have to cooperate…"

She would have answered any question to get him to do what she so desperately wanted.

"Will he take it?" Nejiko whispered to me. Her eyes were deep and dark with pain.

"I don't know," I said. "He just asked to see you, and that you bring it."

She bowed, a neat, graceful bow. Each of them had their own distinctive style of bowing; how much more interesting than a soft handshake instead of a firm one, I thought.

"One moment," she said. "I must dress. I practice in my *yukata*."

Mrs. Harada left, and I waited on the balcony, looking down on the shady green lawn where the men were walking laps in circles, as though in a prison yard. And they were, of course.

I looked away, across to the mountainside. Almost hidden in the forest, I could see the pavilion where Neal had kissed me.

Mr. Phelps was on the phone, arguing with Mrs. Johnson. He waved us away from his desk.

"Prudence, yes, it's a nuisance. But I want to keep things as quiet as possible here, do you understand me?"

He listened, and then continued.

"Then move him to one of the empty rooms on the third floor balcony."

He cocked his head, held the receiver away from his ear. It crackled with her angry response.

"Of course I know your girls are on the fourth floor. But he's not a convicted felon, Prudence. He's a diplomatic prisoner. He's our guest, for the duration. We have an additional inconvenient problem, that's all. Take care of it, please. As instructed."

So he was doing what he had promised Gwendolyn Harada—arranging to separate her from her husband.

Nejiko Suwa sat in the chair by my desk, stroking her violin case. She wore a pleated skirt and white blouse, and looked very young and delicate. When my boss came in, she stood and bowed—not like an artist acknowledging applause as she had the night before, but like a frightened school girl. How much power he has, I realized. Everything was so civilized here, on the surface. It was easy to forget who we were, and who they were.

"Come in, please, Miss Suwa," he said.

She followed him, clasping the violin close.

I leaned back in my chair and listened.

"Sit down please. That was a beautiful performance last night. You are very talented."

"Thank you," she murmured.

"Where were you trained?"

"As a child, growing up in Mejiro, with Anna Bubnova-Ono, a Russian violinist who came to my country after their revolution. She introduced me to Efrem Zimbalist when he visited, and he arranged for me to come to Paris in 1938."

"And I understand Joseph Goebbels gave you your instrument."

His voice was stern.

"Sir, I was most fortunate in my reception in Europe. Two years ago, I was staying with Ambassador Oshima and Lady Ambassador. They are great music lovers, and arranged for me to give a concert with the Berlin Philharmonic. My dressing room was decorated with cherry blossoms—they called me the violinist from the land of the cherry blossoms."

"But what about the violin?" persisted Mr. Phelps. "Was Goebbels at this concert?"

Her voice was always soft. Now it became almost inaudible. I hovered closer to the doorway, though I didn't dare go in. "Minister Goebbels sent regrets to my dressing room. He requested me to meet with him the next day, and it was then he presented me with the violin."

"Which must have been stolen from its rightful owner, I'm sure you realize."

"He said it was his. If I ever learned it belonged to someone else—I would return it. Please, I've kept it safe—through airstrikes, escaping Paris, Berlin. It's all I have—my dearest friend stayed behind in Berlin when we evacuated. He was—he *is* protecting the portraits of the Emperor in the tunnel beneath the Embassy. He offered to keep it for me there, but I couldn't risk leaving it behind." Her voice broke. Who was this left-behind dearest friend to her?

Mr. Phelps said, "And so if its owner has survived, you will return it?"

"I promise."

She must have nodded. My boss continued. "Could you play for me now? Mendelssohn?"

"It has been a long time. He was forbidden, you know."

"Something from the Concerto in E Minor? My wife—my wife played. Plays."

She began. The strains of music were irresistible. I could not resist creeping into his office.

Mr. Phelps listened with a far-away expression. After the music, he removed his glasses and pressed his hand to his eyes.

"You may go," he said softly.

She placed her violin in the case, nestled it into the red velvet; snapped it shut.

I waited for what was coming, the order for her to leave it behind. I hoped he would not ask me to take it from her.

"I may ask you to come again and play for me," he said.

She bowed. "It would be an honor."

"You may go. Take good care of that instrument."

"It is dearer to me than my life," she said.

As we walked down the hill to the hotel, I said, "Your friend in Berlin—you must miss him."

"Very much," she said. "But I cannot speak of him to anyone. His wife is here, you see."

I wanted to ask more then, but did not dare. I wished I could tell her I knew about being separated. About Neal.

But neither of us spoke again.

Chapter Three

The phone on my desk rang. Ada was calling from the lobby switchboard.

"Hazel? We have a Mr. Levy from the Office of Price Administration in Altoona, out to investigate our books. Here! Is Mr. Phelps expecting anyone?" Ada sounded flustered, not like her usual cool-as-a-cucumber self.

Mr. Phelps swiveled in his chair as he spoke to her—clearly irritated, though he always kept his tone level. "Ada, I don't care who he says he is, or who he says he's representing. No, absolutely not. No, we're not admitting anyone without proper authorization from Altoona, and Washington. Have the guards escort him off the property." He slammed down the phone. "Damn. Hazel, I need the Office of Price Administration in Altoona on the line. And get me the list of attendees at the meeting State held here."

"Yes, sir." He had never sworn before!

After the call went through, I rifled through the files for the roster from that meeting.

He was talking very loudly. "Yes, wants in to investigate our books. Claims he's got evidence the hotel and the State Department are violating price controls. He says he was at the meeting before we opened."

I found the list and brought it to him. He nodded thanks, still on the phone, running his finger down the page, stabbing at the offending names. His voice was icy, but I could feel the heat underneath and retreated to my desk in the next room. "Malicious nonsense, sir. No, I won't admit him until you and Washington officially authorize it. Good-bye, sir."

"Hazel!" He yelled, though I was just feet away at my desk in the next room. "Call down to the guard house and tell them not to admit any visitors. I need Assistant Secretary Acheson on the line."

I had never seen him perspiring. Even so, Lytton Phelps managed to sound calm as he spoke to the Secretary. "Yes, sir; misguided vigilante, I suspect. Persistent." Mr. Phelps listened. "Very well, sir. If you think it's necessary. I'll send a letter of invitation to the OPA this afternoon."

My boss stamped into my office. "Call down to Prudence Johnson. Get her up here. Right away."

I dialed the kitchen. "Mrs. Johnson," I said. "Mr. Phelps needs to see you."

"I'm busy with luncheon. I'll be along shortly," she said. Mrs. Johnson considered Mr. Phelps and everyone else to be interlopers on her domain. It didn't seem to matter whether we were from Bedford, Washington, D.C., or Japan by way of Berlin. She'd grumbled openly about my boss, ever since he had ordered her to move Takeo Harada to the third floor.

"Sorry, he said right away," I said.

The cook appeared in my office, glowering. "Where's the fire?" she demanded.

My boss came out to meet her. "Thanks, Prudence. I know you're busy, but representatives of the OPA want to audit our books. I've sent them on their way, for today, but   Assistant Secretary Acheson deems it necessary to authorize the inquiry," Mr. Phelps explained.

"Check my books?" she replied. She was so indignant, bubbles of spittle actually frothed on her lips. "Outrageous! A waste of time. We haven't done anything wrong—way too busy to cook the books, as well as these meals with nothing!"

"I know, Prudence," he said, "But I just need your assurance that there have been no initial cost over-runs, that you are staying within the budget and ration points."

"Of course, sir," she said, aggrieved.

"And no one on your staff has engaged in any bartering or black market activity for local commodities."

"Certainly not."

"Well then, nothing to be worried about."

"This is nonsense," said Mrs. Johnson. "I'm doing everything properly."

"We all know it's not popular to have the detainees here. In fact, I know you're not keen on it yourself. We must expect scrutiny. I am grateful you're here, doing a fine job, and I know there will be nothing irregular for them to find. However, Secretary Acheson has ordered us to comply."

The woman, so angry the stiff gray waves of her hair bristled, said, "Well, if we're talking irregularities, sir, well moving that Japanese man up to the third floor—I just don't like having a prisoner right below the girls living in."

"Hazel, do you feel unsafe?"

"No, sir." She glared at me. But none of the Japanese frightened me—except Ambassador Oshima.

"It's a necessary stop-gap, Prudence. Remember, our guests are diplomats. I don't want any unpleasantness with the British Embassy on top of everything else. And I do not want to hear anything more about this matter."

"I'll quit if you don't like the way I'm doing my job, sir."

"Prudence, don't take this so personally."

"I don't appreciate having my judgment and my management questioned."

"We have a complicated operation, Prudence. Formalities. Protocol. I have utmost confidence in you."

"If anything is out of line, if there is anything for this investigator to find, I'll quit."

She marched out of the Cottage.

Mr. Phelps shrugged off his seersucker jacket. "Hazel," he said. "A letter. To the Honorable Chester Bowles, Administrator of the OPA. Copy to Assistant Secretary Acheson. Ready?" My boss was drumming his fingers on the desk, impatient. He began as soon as I sat down with my pad.

"*A representative of the Altoona office of the OPA called at the Bedford Springs Hotel today and applied for admission, alleging that he was in possession of information that the Hotel management and the Department of State were violating OPA regulations by paying prices higher than ceiling prices for food served to the detainees. As the Department representative in charge, I have standing instructions not to admit any persons without advance authorization from Washington. In accord with those instructions, the representative from Altoona was not admitted.*

From the start of negotiations with the Hotel management in advance of the detainees' arrival, as well as subsequently to the direct staff since the actual arrival of the detainees, we have made clear the State Department's requirement that all OPA regulations must be respected, including avoiding buying on the local market commodities in short supply, limiting ration points per detainee to the allowance for ordinary civilians. The Hotel management representative in charge assures me there have been no violations. We have, as you know, limited the ration points per detainee to the allowance for ordinary civilians despite the fact the OPA regulations permit 1.6 ration points per meal for persons residing in hotels. The Hotel does, as agreed, operate on a 10 percent overhead commission. We support a joint investigation to ensure there have been neither overpayments on food nor any resultant, fraudulent inflation of the commission.

If the management or staff of the Hotel has violated any OPA regulations, they are in contempt of our instructions. We are prepared to facilitate a prompt investigation to determine whether there is any validity to the Altoona individual's charges. I look forward to your comments and instructions on the foregoing."

I typed up the letter on the Underwood Noiseless, black and shiny as patent leather, much nicer than the machines I had learned on at the high school. My father had not wanted me to take the business course; it would be useless at Bryn Mawr, he'd said. What would he think now, about my job? He would like Mr. Phelps, I imagined, and the way my boss managed to remain dignified and courteous under pressure.

The OPA visit was scheduled for the end of the week. Phelps offered my help to Prudence Johnson with the necessary document production. She refused, as though we had instigated the investigation and were leagued against her. "I have a hotel to run. I don't have time for this nonsense," she muttered.

"Let her rant," he said to me. "We're a safety valve. A lightning rod."

The man from the OPA had a deeply lined face and (to my amazement and Ada's amusement) the startling black hair of someone much younger—my first encounter with a man vain enough to dye his hair. My boss met with him privately. After he left, Lytton Phelps made a point of thanking Mrs. Johnson for her work, and for having such accurate documentation. "Everything proved to be in perfect order."

"Of course, sir," she said coldly. "Just doing my job—as always."

But there was a glint of satisfaction in her steel blue eyes at this vindication, and afterward she seemed less resentful of my boss.

Over supper in the staff dining room one of the local girls, Wanda, was full of excitement. Her boyfriend Andy, who had been a prisoner in Germany for six months, had safely, miraculously, arrived home. He would pick her up tonight after work. I was ashamed of how jealous I felt.

"You won't believe how thin he is, but he's all in one piece!"

"Neal's next," Cora whispered to me, "I just know it."

Wanda's good fortune should have encouraged me, but I felt envious, as though Andy had used up one of a limited quota of safe returns, as though Wanda had grabbed the only gold ring on the carousel. I dreaded being there, when he came, having to watch and listen while Wanda flaunted him.

Joe seemed to read my mind. "There's a speaker at the Rotary tonight. A reporter who worked in Japan. Anyone want to go?"

"Yes," I said—eager to get away, and curious about what this reporter would say.

The Rotary met in the basement fellowship hall of the Presbyterian Church on the Square. We arrived late and stood against the wall; every seat was taken. It was very hot in the windowless room. The speaker, a Mr. Young, seemed to have hypnotized the audience. Thin and agitated, he paced restlessly and pointed his finger at the crowd. He sounded like the revival preacher I'd heard one summer when Neal and I snuck into the tent pitched by the river.

"The Japs shut my paper down, arrested me, held me in solitary confinement! I was lucky to get out alive. You have a Trojan horse in your midst! Wake up! Wake up to the danger! Oshima was Hitler's best friend and advisor, and a general in the Imperial Army. Making him an ambassador doesn't mean he's not still a general. Trust me, this man is the one personally responsible for the Japanese plan to conquer the world."

I hadn't heard that before. But even if it were true, wasn't Oshima's direct connection to Hitler to our advantage? That was why the Japanese would do anything to get him back, after all. *Because* he was Hitler's friend, they would release General Wainwright. Release Neal. Hitler was dead and we had his best friend. That was the point, after all! This man was dead wrong.

He was ranting, but in a soft nasal voice that sent a chill down my spine.

"You have a nest of serpents, a gang of Jap admirals, generals, colonels and navy captains, right down the road at your precious Bedford Springs Hotel." The man walked down the aisle, glaring at us. "They traveled to Pennsylvania in air conditioned Pullman cars, with unlimited personal effects, like visiting royalty. And now they're in the lap of luxury."

He returned to the podium, took a sip of water, and continued. "And mark my words, the management of the hotel is cleaning up. Taxpayer money, your money, my money, fitted out the hotel with new oriental rugs and fine furniture. Getting $30 a day for each prisoner. Giving them unlimited access to the telephone and radio. It's a disgrace to the good people of this community that some of you are willing to work out there, wait on the Japs hand and foot, serve them gourmet food from Washington, sell them perfumed hair tonic and silk kimonos, leather shoes right in the hotel gift shop."

"That's ridiculous! He doesn't know what he's talking about," I hissed to Joe.

A man in the row in front of us turned and looked at me. "Quiet!"

"If I were you, I'd run the Japs out of town. I'd tar and feather them. And the collaborators," Mr. Young said.

The man in front of us turned around again, and looked right at me.

"We're leaving," Joe said, pulling me to my feet.

Frightened, I followed him into the square. It was a relief to be in the cool air. We stood in the Square by the Civil War monument.

"He's whipping things up. It could get ugly," Joe said.

"But he makes them sound dangerous, and makes us sound like—like we're traitors for working there. Someone should tell them he's wrong."

"Not us. Let's go."

"But they're not a gang of generals!" I protested, as we walked to the car.

"Drop it, Hazel, he's nasty. He's exaggerating, maybe—but after all, Oshima's a general. And Hitler's friend. They're our enemies alright. Done evil stuff. Don't you forget it."

"Not the children. Hating everyone Japanese is like something Hitler would have done."

We drove back to the hotel in a heavy silence. The tension sparked by the Rotary meeting lingered; I imagined shadows creeping out of the forest on Evitt's Mountain, imagined a lynch mob of locals coming after all of us—Japanese and staff alike.

Joe parked beside the garage.

"He's a hatemonger, Joe."

"Well, there's a lot to hate. Just don't forget why we're doing this."

"I don't!" I flounced off. Somehow Mr. Young's vitriol had even stirred something ugly between me and Joe.

Upstairs under the eaves, Cora's door was open. She sprawled on her bed, doing her nails. It was so hot her blonde hair had curled into tight corkscrews.

"How was the talk?" she asked, looking up, holding the little brush above her nail.

"A bunch of lies about what's going on here," I said.

"Tell me about it. I'm almost finished. I'll do your nails."

I sat on the edge of her bed, watching her stroke the red onto her nails. The sweet smell was overpowering in the stuffy attic room.

"Did Andy come?"

She nodded.

"Did he say what it was like?"

"We didn't talk about it. I don't think he wanted to." She waved her hand through the air, drying the nails. I stood up.

"Wait, I can do yours now."

"No thanks," I said. "I'm turning in."

I undressed and put on my nightgown. As I rubbed cold cream on my face, I looked at Neal's photograph. Say something. Send me a sign.

***

"Sir," I said to Lytton Phelps the next morning, "I heard this reporter at the Rotary. He said awful things, some of it lies, about what's going on here."

He nodded. "You went to hear Young? They love him in the *Hearst News*. Being read all over the country. We'll have some damage control to do."

The phone rang as I uncovered my typewriter.

"State Department," said Ada. "Mr. Clattenberg for him."

The phone rang all morning in shrill demanding volleys—everyone, from local officials to Congressmen, questioning how the detention was being handled. A local Representative, a Mr. Buell, demanded to see first-hand what was going on, to ensure the safety of his constituents. My boss handled the call politely, but was fuming when he got off the phone.

"He's threatening to go to Truman, says he wouldn't put up with any red tape. He insists on coming out to do an inspection," my boss said. "Get me Acheson, please, Hazel."

Phelps paced back and forth like a bull on a chain until Ada got the call through.

"Sir, if we don't get an effective retraction out, get the record corrected immediately; we won't have a chance to accomplish what we need to with this swap. We're fighting psychological warfare here, and you know there's nothing easier to run off the rails."

Later, he dictated a letter to Secretary Acheson, rebutting Young's allegations.

The detainees travelled in plain coaches, bringing strictly limited personal effects. Hotel staff provides only minimal services to satisfy the terms of the Geneva Convention. Food from standard purveyors in Pittsburgh does not and will not exceed 50 ration points per person per month, and that is only one third of the customary hotel allowance. Meals are served cafeteria style, and staff provides only the services necessary to maintain the hotel. The inmates do not have private radios; they are permitted to buy approved newspapers, toothpaste and soap at the hotel shop—running a hotel tab from their private funds on deposit at a local bank. No resident may exceed fifty dollars per month. Neither luxury furniture nor china is in use; the furniture and china of the hotel suffered quite a bit of depreciation so it has been necessary to make some piecemeal interim replacements with second hand items. Some carpets— paid for by the hotel management—have been installed, but only on cement portions of the floor which are not suitable for elderly persons, women, and children.

He read and signed my typescript. "I want this in the afternoon mail to Washington," he said.

The next day, Congressman Buell and his secretary arrived. I had expected someone much more impressive. Buell was so short and stout that Ada, whispering, called him "Mr. Two by Four."

But Mr. Phelps welcomed the visitors pleasantly, as though it were a social call. He explained the daily schedule while I served coffee and Prudence Johnson's sweet rolls. She must have used a good part of the sugar ration on those treats! I saved one and nibbled it at my desk while the men talked in the next room.

"The detainees rise at 7 a.m., breakfast is served at 8, roll-call and room inspection at 9."

"Who carries out the roll-call and inspection?"

"Members of the Border Patrol. Lunch is served at noon, dinner at five—preceded by a second roll-call. Meals are prepared strictly according to available ration points and the Immigration and Naturalization menu guide. Curfew is at 10 p.m."

"I would think it advisable to have a final roll-call at curfew," said the Congressman. "Remember the German POW who escaped from a camp in Emmitsburg."

"Our detainees are of a higher class, and racially distinct, of course. They could not pass or mingle in the populace, so escape is out of the question. And a good number are children; they retire before the final curfew. A roll-call would be disruptive. Remember, these are diplomatic detainees."

The Congressman looked skeptical.

"And what do they do all day?"

"Very little, sir. Recreational facilities are, of course, off limits. Walk for exercise, within the compound."

"Why not put the men to work, in the orchards near here. They've done that in Emmitsburg."

"Well, sir, as you pointed out, there was an escape there, connected with the agricultural work release. And again, our detainees are diplomats."

I could detect a note of quiet pleasure in my boss's voice, almost as though he were playing a game with the Congressman, and winning.

"I want to meet him. The General," Mr. Buell said.

"He'll be at lunch. Perhaps you'd like to sample our menu?" Mr. Phelps suggested.

The Ambassador was seated with his usual inner circle of attachés. "Ambassador," said Mr. Phelps, approaching the table, "let me present Congressman Buell."

Oshima, immaculate as always in a fine suit, rose and bowed, giving his close-lipped, insolent smile. Years later, historians would consider him more Nazi than the Nazis. But ironically, Oshima was also the Nazis' Achilles heel. No one—not Phelps, not Oshima himself—knew it then, but the arrogant Ambassador had played an unwitting part in breaking the Axis stranglehold: cryptographers broke his coded messages from Berlin to Tokyo, thus gaining invaluable information about Hitler's plans.

After meeting the Ambassador, the Congressman picked at the meal, Mrs. Johnson's creamed salt cod on biscuits. "How do you keep tabs on him? Has the Navy's radio equipment been removed? Could they be transmitting?"

"The Navy's equipment is gone. The detainees have no radios—complete fabrication in Mr. Young's article. We only have English language newspapers in the hotel shop—and one Japanese language newspaper approved by the State Department. It's reviewed by censors beforehand."

"Telephone? Mail?" Buell demanded.

"No telephone use. Mail is censored, and must be in English. The Ambassador's assistants—Mr. Ono, Fujiyama, and Yamanaka—are among the translators. Those who cannot speak English submit complaints to them."

"Complaints? They have no right to complain."

"Well, I take your point. However, we must handle everything in strictest accord with Geneva, or it could have adverse effects on our prisoners over there."

We walked along the porch and then downstairs to the hotel shop, our commissary. The Congressman inspected the limited inventory as though expecting contraband, but found only the officially permitted paper, stamps, toothpaste, bath soap, cigarettes.

"Cigarettes?" Buell looked shocked.

"We must sell anything that Federal prisoners are allowed, that's the regulation," said my boss. "And our staff and guards buy smokes too, of course."

"How do the Japs pay for all this?"

Lytton Phelps answered as we walked back to the porch. "The detainees brought whatever money they could out of Germany—in a variety of currencies: Swiss francs, Reich marks, the new French franc, old French francs, even some dollars. The monies are on deposit in town; each detainee is authorized an allowance equivalent to fifty dollars a month. However, one problem we're facing is with French francs. You see, the French government has required all old francs to be exchanged for new francs."

Congressman Buell nodded, looking glazed. I suspected my boss was intentionally flooding him with information.

"You see, Congressman, some detainees, already in custody in Europe when the decree went into effect, have money only in old francs. Quite complicated, actually."

"I want to see where the Ambassador sleeps," Buell said, interrupting.

"Of course."

We climbed up to the first balcony. Phelps rapped on the door, and Mrs. Oshima opened it, bowing as though to a guest instead of an intruder. Phelps slipped his shoes off before entering and left them outside according to the detainees' custom. Congressman Buell and his secretary wore theirs inside. I waited on the balcony, more afraid of the Ambassador than curious. The sound of violin and piano music wafted up from the lounge below.

"What's that?" asked Congressman Buell, emerging from the bedroom and starting down the steps, following the music.

My boss and I hurried after him.

The stout man was winded by his hastiness. Buell stood on the threshold of the lounge, face florid, catching his breath as he stared in. Nejiko saw him; lifted her bow and fell silent. Mrs. Harada played on, oblivious or defiant.

The Congressman's already florid face turned scarlet as he observed her.

"You allow this—staff fraternizing, concertizing with the prisoners?"

He'd mistaken Gwendolyn Harada for one of us, for a member of the staff.

"They are both detainees, Congressman," said Mr. Phelps. "The pianist is married to one of the General's attachés."

Gwendolyn Harada's back stiffened. She dropped her hands and swiveled on the piano bench, confronting us.

"An unrightful prisoner, sir. A British subject. Awaiting intervention from my ambassador," she said.

"You are a disgrace to your country," Buell said, and stalked away.

Gwendolyn Harada stared after him; the color drained from her face. But her green eyes snapped and I remembered the fox Neal and I had found once, trapped and furious.

In the lobby, Buell prepared to depart.

"Overall, Phelps, I've found things in order. But I have to say, I am shocked and dismayed by this laxity in permitting such entertainment as I've just witnessed. It was clearly stated that the prisoners would have no access to recreational facilities. And here, contrary to your assurances to me, I find them music making as though at Chautauqua! My constituents would be most displeased."

"I understand your point, sir. I will rectify the situation."

After Buell left, Phelps returned to the lounge. The women had resumed their practicing.

My boss hesitated on the threshold for a moment. Then he sighed, straightened his shoulders, and strode to the piano.

"Ladies," he said. "Excuse me, but in light of the Congressman's objection, I must ask that you stop."

Mrs. Harada lifted long fingers from the keyboard with an elaborate flourish and shuffled her music on the stand. "Well, let us know when he's gone so we can get back to work. We were planning a lovely program for after dinner."

"I'm sorry, Madam. I will have to ask that you give me your music, and refrain from using the piano henceforth. Miss Suwa, I will take your instrument into safe-keeping."

Nejiko's hands trembled as she placed her violin in its velvet lined case.

Gwendolyn Harada dropped her music on the bench and slammed the keyboard shut. "When I speak with my Ambassador he'll hear about this."

My boss tapped his fingers together and straightened his tie. It was unlike him to fidget. "Hazel, take the violin, the music. We will keep everything for the duration. Mrs. Harada, I need to have a word with you. Please come with me."

Nejiko Suwa closed the clasps on the violin case and stroked the cover. "Take good care of it, please. It is the most precious thing in the world to me. My life, my future depends on it." The young woman held the case out to me.

I wasn't brave enough, then, to protest, to defy my boss. I should have begged him to let her keep it, refused to be part of this. But I accepted the instrument. "We'll keep it safe," I promised. I carried it close to me, as I followed my boss and Mrs. Harada back to the office.

He took it from me, and locked it in the safe. Then he shut the pocket doors. I stepped as close as I could, to listen.

"I spoke with your Embassy. They can be of no assistance with a divorce, and said that your request for return to England is highly unlikely to be granted."

"But my daughter and I are refugees at this point."

"Hardly, Mrs. Harada. Rather enemy aliens. No, you must expect to be returned to Japan."

"It's not a return! I've never lived there."

"You married Mr. Harada. You lived in Berlin."

"Please, help us. There must be something you can do. At least—permit me to contact the Embassy directly, make my case. Put my family in touch with them."

"It is out of my hands," he said. His exasperated, final tone signaled that even his patience was done. I hurried back to my desk just before he slid the door open.

"Hazel, take Mrs. Harada back, and ask Mrs. Johnson to make her some tea."

"I'm so sorry," I said, as we walked toward the hotel. "I have loved listening to you play. I will truly miss it."

"Oh, I'm not surprised. They take everything away. First our books, now this."

"Your books? We haven't taken any books." I realized as I spoke that, oddly, I'd not seen anyone reading a book since they'd arrived.

"They pawed through everything in Le Havre, took what they fancied. And confiscated all our books. Said we'd get them back in New York. We didn't of course. Not even the children's school books. They kept everything—German, English, Japanese. Burned, for all I know."

No wonder the men lined up so eagerly for the few newspapers permitted to be sold in the commissary—desperate for news, and desperate for reading.

"Do a favor for me?" She spoke softly but put a strong, imperious hand on my arm, forcing me to a standstill. "Mail a letter for me—a personal matter, I just don't want it to go through the censors."

I thought of my father. *Obey the higher law, the law of conscience,* he used to say. *Ask forgiveness, not permission.* Do it, he would say. Love your friend, love your enemy. And she, after all, was really neither friend nor enemy, just another woman caught in this war.

But I thought also of losing my job, of returning to Grace McKee's to wait out the end of the war—to wait in idleness for news of Neal. To pretend to hope. And then when the news came? The bad news I was almost certain of? I had to stay here. Somehow, as long as I was here, as long as the Japanese were here—there was some kind of hope.

"I'm sorry, I can't do that for you. I might lose my job." For the second time that day, failing to be brave enough to follow the voice of my conscience.

She released my arm as though dismissing me, rejecting me.

As we continued in silence down the hill, I struggled between shame and trying to excuse myself. After all, as everyone said, she had *chosen* to marry a Japanese.

And I had chosen to marry Neal. Would Gwendolyn Harada and I have chosen differently, if we had known what was coming?

"I'll bring tea to you in the lounge," I said. At least I could offer her that.

When I arrived with the tea tray, I found her alone, sitting on the piano bench. She'd opened the keyboard but did not touch the keys.

"Here's your tea."

She closed the keyboard and turned toward me. Perhaps if she had begged me again to mail the letter, I could have continued to resist. But her silence, her expression of bottomless weariness and pain, worked on me. And perhaps, perhaps, through some sort of magic, some law of fairness, an act of kindness would work in Neal's favor.

"Hide the letter in the piano bench," I whispered.

Her eyes glistened with tears. Without a word, she unclasped her pearl necklace and offered it to me. "Here," she said. "With my eternal gratitude."

"No," I said. "No, I don't want anything." Though the pearls were tempting, lustrous and gleaming in her cupped palm. "It's the right thing to do. That's all."

"The necklace means nothing to me anymore. It's Japanese," she said ruefully. "He gave it to me." But the gentle way she fondled the pearls and a catch in her voice told me how much she still cared for the necklace—and for him. It had never occurred to me—the possibility you could be angry at someone, and still love him.

"Save it for your daughter," I said. "Charlotte will want them. She should have the necklace. My mother is gone. I cherish her things."

She looked at me, furious. "My daughter must forget him."

"I can't take your necklace," I said.

After curfew sounded and the Japanese marched up to bed, I returned to the deserted lounge. Opening the piano bench, I discovered not one but two letters. And a small satin pouch. I knew what it held—the necklace.

Leave the pearls, I scolded myself.

But I slipped the pouch into my pocket with the letters and hurried to my room like a thief.

I locked my door and before even reading the letters, I tried on the necklace. The pearls felt soft as silk, resting along my clavicle. I admired my reflection, promising myself I'd just keep the necklace overnight. Just hold the pearls tonight for safekeeping—like Mr. Phelps keeping the violin. If I left them in the piano bench, anyone might steal them. Hiding the pearls deep in my bureau drawer, behind Neal's letters, I turned to the letters.

Her handwriting was ornate—all slopes and curlicues, a strange ornamental style of script, not what I had learned from the chalk board at the Common School in Bedford.

One was addressed to the British Ambassador in Washington, and one to Mr. and Mrs. Christopher E. Mason in someplace called Kensington, in London, England.

I would mail them, as I promised. But first, didn't I have an obligation to ensure there was no treachery? Carefully, delicately, I pried open the flap on the first envelope.

Bedford Springs, 2nd August
Dearly Beloved Mother and Father,
We are here at Bedford, in Pennsylvania, in the States. I am longing for you, praying you have survived the war, and can find it in your hearts to forgive me. I hear reports that the bombing in London was terrible, and that there is little to eat. For us at the end in Berlin conditions were very difficult—Tiergartenstrasse and the Embassy right in the center of the heaviest bombing. The grand hotels—the Esplanade, the Excelsior, the Furstenhof, are gone. We heard the final concert at the Philharmonic, in April, just before being evacuated. Electricity turned on just for the concert. Beethoven's Violin Concerto in D major. It was freezing in the hall, Charlotte turned positively blue. We walked to the concert, and home—no trams for months. I hadn't ventured outside for ever so long. The ruined city looked like the end of the world. The Ambassador ordered us to evacuate. A few attachés stayed behind to guard the imperial portraits in an underground bunker at the Embassy. I thought Takeo might volunteer—he's fanatic about the Emperor, and desperate for the

Ambassador to recognize him. But he didn't, and Oshima didn't order him to stay.. Oshima is a cruel man, but at least he didn't do that. It was too late really to get away; we were almost killed in the streets of Berlin, and then Americans captured us. They treated us miserably and, after a beastly crossing on a military ship, we arrived in New York. In spite of everything, Charlotte was so excited to see the Statue of Liberty. She remembered seeing the little one, in Paris, on our last holiday. Liberty. There's been no liberty for us. They held us like common criminals at Ellis Island. Sent us here like luggage. Finally we ended up here in Pennsylvania, in the middle of nowhere. My situation is quite desperate, darlings. They're sending us to Japan. Please forgive everything. You were right, Daddy. I've asked for a divorce. My greatest desire in life now is to return to England and put all of this behind us. Charlotte has grown up so fast over these war years. She's thirteen, quite the young lady! You will not recognize her, Mother. There's so much more to say, but really this is just to say, please, please ask our M.P. for help. Ask anyone you can think of with any pull. Please. Please.

With much love and thanks forever,
Gwen

The next letter was briefer, to her ambassador.

I ask for your help. I have committed no crime except the youthful indiscretion of falling in love with and marrying a Japanese man when we were both students at Oxford.

We met and married in 1930, between wars, in another world and time. My husband entered the Japanese diplomatic corps, stationed in London. As you know, the relationship between England and Japan was vastly different then. Why, for example, just before being stationed to Berlin in 1937, my husband and I were among the official guests of Prince and Princess Chichibu, who had come at royal invitation to represent their Emperor at King George VI's coronation. The Prince and Princess were honored guests, the very first to enter Westminster Abbey that day, the very first to be seated, since they represented the longest existing imperial line. I was proud to be with them. How could I, a young, naïve girl, ever have foretold, just months later, war would break out between Japan and China, and I would be stranded in Germany? Please, for the sake of my daughter, let me be English again. Let me come home.

Respectfully yours,
Mrs. Gwendolyn Harada, née Mason

Ashamed of myself for prying, I re-sealed the envelopes. Tomorrow I would mail the letters, and return the necklace.

Chapter Four

The next morning, I hid the letters in my pocket. I tried on the pearls and admired myself in the mirror, enjoyed the smooth orbs against my skin—one last time. Then I hid them in my pocket as well. After delivering my boss's breakfast, I went to find her.

Gwendolyn Harada sat on the porch, no one nearby except two Japanese women, rocking. Their children were playing at their feet, whining a little, tired and cranky already.

Mrs. Harada looked pale and exhausted and, for the first time, a little shabby. Her dress was wrinkled, and the spectator pumps were scuffed and dirty.

"I can't accept this," I said softly, and held out the pouch which held the pearls.

"It was a thank you," she said. "Not a bribe."

"Keep it for Charlotte."

"No. It only reminds me of how foolish I was. Better not to have any souvenirs."

"But you still love him," I whispered.

She shook her head. Her voice sounded bitter. "Oh, love. I was so young. So naive. Guess how we met?"

"How?"

"At a peace rally in Oxford of all places, waiting in a queue to sign a resolution that we would never take up arms. It was my last term at Lady Margaret Hall. He signed his name just before me. The most beautiful man I'd ever seen."

Beautiful is not a word I had ever associated with a man. But, in his case, Gwendolyn Harada was right. And ever since, occasionally—in a theater lobby, or an airport lounge—I encounter a Japanese man of a certain age, with exquisite, balanced features, and think, *beautiful.*

Gwendolyn continued. "A *coup de foudre.* We spent every moment we could together. He proposed to me in the garden at Magdalen. He warned me, his parents had selected a Japanese bride for him—a picture bride, they called them."

"Like—a mail-order bride?"

"There were so many young Japanese men in England, then. So many eligible Japanese bachelors whose parents wanted them to marry Japanese girls."

"But he didn't take his picture bride."

"No. He cabled his parents about me. His father ordered him home. Takeo refused. It was all so romantic, so thrilling. So stupid."

"But you loved each other."

She looked at me with a strange expression, almost as though I had said something amusing. "Well, we went to London, to tell my parents. My father had Japanese acquaintances—bankers, businessmen. Nothing to worry about, I told Takeo. But when Takeo asked for my hand, my father ordered him to leave the house. And I left too."

"So you married him, even though they said not to?" It seemed so brave.

"A hurry-up registry wedding in Oxford, just the two of us.

A lovely day, actually. We went out to the Trout afterward, and punting."

"Punting?"

But she wasn't listening to me. She was watching the Fukuzawa baby toddle past along the veranda, trailed by her mother. Kiyoko had just learned to walk, delighting everyone, American and Japanese, like a mascot. The baby's father, Shintaro Fukuzawa, was one of the inner circle of attachés who always ate with the Ambassador.

The baby collapsed on her round bottom and howled. Mrs. Fukuzawa scooped her up and walked away.

Gwendolyn looked after them. "Takeo and Shintaro began together at the Embassy in London. We were friends, at first, all posted to Berlin together in '37. Chamberlain was still talking appeasement."

"How old was Charlotte?"

"Five. My mother came, secretly, to Kensington Gardens to say good-bye. I should have left him then, and stayed. In Berlin he was passed over—never demoted, but never promoted. Because of me. We've ruined each other's lives."

"Don't say that," I said.

She shook her head. "It's true, my dear. I expected Oshima would abandon us in Berlin, when the city fell and the Embassy evacuated in May. It was like piling into lifeboats on the Titanic. Japanese are ruthless when they're desperate. Don't let the courtesy, the bowing, fool you."

"When people are frightened, no one is at their best, I suppose."

She laughed again. "Who taught you to have such faith in human nature?"

"My father," I said.

"You should introduce him to Ambassador Oshima."

"He's dead."

"Oh, pardon me."

"He was—we're Quakers."

"Pacifists?"

"He was."

"Wise man." she said.

"But my, my husband wasn't—isn't—a pacifist, or Quaker. He's missing. In the Pacific."

She looked at me, solemn. "I am so sorry."

"Tell me what it was like," I said. I was afraid to hear more, but I had to hear more. "When Berlin fell and you—evacuated."

"Horrific. Fighting in the streets, boy soldiers throwing bricks at the cavalcade of cars from the Embassy. Air so filled with smoke it hurt to breathe. And the countryside, the orchards where Takeo took us hiking at blossom time? Blasted away. Gaping holes where houses were. I kept Charlotte's head in my lap the whole way. I didn't let her see. But she could smell it. Burned flesh. Rotting cadavers. We've cursed her life."

"What happened—it wasn't your fault."

She wasn't listening to me, lost in her memories.

"The tanks, the Americans, stopped us before we got to Switzerland. The soldiers called me a whore. Treated me worse than the Japanese."

Ada called from the doorway.

"Hazel—Mr. Phelps just called down to the desk. He needs you in the office."

I broke away and ran up the hill. The pearls were still in my pocket, with her letters. All through the morning, as I typed and filed, I felt the weight of my secrets. Before lunch I date-stamped her envelopes with the Special Projects Division seal and buried them in the bag of approved mail. I'd lost my appetite and skipped lunch, climbing the stairs to my room to hide the necklace deep in the back corner of my top bureau drawer. Neal looked at me from the picture frame with his unchanging resolute expression. "Well, if you know so much, tell me, what's the right thing to do!" I said.

That evening Joe invited me to play ping pong for the first time in days. We hadn't played since the night of the reporter at the Rotary. He'd asked once or twice, but I'd refused.

"I saw you with the English woman," Joe said, lobbing the ball at me with a vicious slice.

I slapped it back over the net. "She's lonely. I'm sorry for her, especially now that she has no music. It was harmless, letting them play. I don't like that congressman."

"Hazel, he's right. Rules are rules. No recreation. And she's married to a Jap." He sounded like Buell, like Phelps, like all of them.

"Some rules are wrong. Did you know they took their books away in France and never gave them back, like they promised? That's not right."

"Don't get started on what's right and wrong. Think of what they've done."

"Well, exactly what has Mrs. Harada done? What have the children done? None of this is their fault."

"So talk to the boss, if you want. Use your influence," he said. "I never expected you'd become such a Jap-lover."

"Don't use that word. I'm not a Jap-lover. I just believe people should be treated right. And maybe I will talk to Phelps," I said. "My father let his prisoners read; taught some of them, even. He said the mind needs exercise as well as the body. No matter what they've done, people deserve to be treated like people."

"That's not how the Japs are treating their prisoners." He didn't say Neal's name; he didn't need to.

"Two wrongs don't make a right." How had my friend become an adversary, a bully I had to face down?

"All I'm saying, Hazel, is be careful. People could get the wrong idea—about you. That's not going to do anyone any good."

"No one asked you to look out for me."

"Neal did, as a matter of fact. Remember?"

It was dangerous, to think of that moment, that train platform in Cumberland. I might cry.

"If he was so worried, he shouldn't have gone away."

"You don't mean that," he said. "I'm just asking you to stop and think. Please, Hazel."

"I am thinking," I said.

"Not clearly."

"Shut up! Don't talk to me like you're my father or something." I dropped my paddle on the table and stamped off.

"Why did they confiscate their books?" I asked Mr. Phelps the next morning.

Startled, he looked up from breaking the yolks of his poached eggs. "What?"

"In Le Havre."

"They confiscated all the non-essential baggage, Hazel. Golf clubs, skis, cameras. Found a few swords, even some guns."

"But books are essential." I gestured to the photograph of his daughters, two blonde girls beneath a Christmas tree. "You'd want your daughters to have something to read if they were prisoners." His daughters lived in New York with their mother. He wrote to them every week.

"The Red Cross is trying to trace the books actually, and tried to borrow some from the library in the Japanese Embassy in Washington, but the Army intelligence department needed those books."

"Whatever for? At least we could get them English books."

"Things must go through channels."

"But why—we have the whole Bedford County Library just down the road. I could bring books here from the library."

"A generous impulse." He sighed, sounding weary. "But people

in town would object, misconstrue."

"They shouldn't. That's just not fair."

"We've had enough trouble." I had learned to tell when his almost inexhaustible patience was about to run out; I heard it in his slightly too even tone.

"What if I just let the English woman's daughter borrow my own books?"

Mr. Phelps removed his glasses, rubbing the bridge of his nose. "Very well. But be careful not to make a special case."

I'd noticed how Charlotte always stood a little apart—marked by her appearance, her poor Japanese: too old to join the younger children playing in the sand of the horse-shoe pit; shunned by the few adolescent girls who had coalesced into a clique led by Teruko Motono, whose father had served as the Japanese Ambassador to the Vichy Government. Charlotte especially needed books. Charlotte could not wait for things to go through channels.

"Thank you!" I said.

"Don't get too attached," he warned.

And so Charlotte became the first of my surrogate children; she started my habit of occasionally caring, perhaps too much, about certain students or young faculty.

I returned to my desk, uncovered my typewriter. Someone knocked.

"Please?" It was the elderly man, Mr. Toshio Takano, the one who had told me about the Firefly Festival. He bowed and entered. Mr. Takano dressed a little differently than most of the men. He wore soft, loose trousers, a short silk jacket, and always his black wool beret rather than the European suits and homburgs Oshima and his circle favored. I'd seen him often on the porch, a cluster of children at his feet, folding paper into amazing shapes—flowers, birds, animals—like a magician entertaining at a party.

According to the dossier I'd read, he emigrated from Japan in

1934, leaving for Paris where he worked as head chef of a restaurant called Le Jardin Japonais. Later he served the Japanese Ambassador in Paris, married a French woman, and had a son. Finally, he was ordered to Berlin to cook for Oshima. His family remained behind in France.

I eavesdropped; Mr. Takano's English was excellent, though he spoke with a faint French accent, like the violinist.

"I have my savings here, held in the local bank, in the old French francs. If there would be some way to find out where my wife and son are, to get funds to them, I would be most grateful."

"Inquiries are pending regarding this matter, on your behalf, with the Red Cross and the Swiss Legation."

On his way out, the little man paused beside my desk, pulled a square of red paper from his jacket pocket and deftly folded it— presenting me with a flower. Next, like a magician transforming a scarf into a dove, he creased a white paper into a bird.

"A crane, for you, mademoiselle," he said, with a slight bow. "In my country, it is customary to fold golden cranes for good fortune. I have no gold paper, I regret."

Just at that moment, Prudence Johnson arrived for her weekly meeting with Phelps to review orders, rations, and shortages. Since their mutual truce after the inspection by the OPA, they had settled into a respectful sort of teamwork.

Mr. Takano bowed. "Madam, permit me to express my gratitude by assisting in the kitchen. I would be honored to be of use."

"What?" she said. Occasionally, she had a slight tremor; now suddenly her head began to tremble violently.

My boss stepped into the room. "It's a thought. You're always telling me you're short-handed, Prudence. Mr. Takano trained in Paris."

"I don't want any Japanese loose with knives in my kitchen."

Mr. Takano cocked his head slightly and wrinkled his forehead.

He almost looked amused.

"Now, does this man look threatening to you? A professional chef. They use German prisoners in the kitchen at Emmitsburg."

"And we know how that turned out—one of them ran off with a local girl," she retorted.

"Somehow I doubt Mr. Takano will be eloping with your Cora," my boss smiled.

"Is this an order?" she asked, glaring.

"A request, Prudence," said my boss. "Haven't you been saying your girls are worked to the bone?"

"At your service," Mr. Takano said to her, with a low bow.

"Come along," she said, grudgingly.

Later, when I carried Mr. Phelps's tray down to the kitchen, I found Mrs. Johnson and the Japanese man standing over a basket of radishes from the garden. He held one between thumb and forefinger, turning it back and forth. "Beautiful," he said. "Might I ask to show you something? It would require a small knife."

Warily, Mrs. Johnson held a paring knife, glancing at me as though to say, "I told you so. If we're all killed, it's on Mr. Phelps's watch."

The man's pudgy fingers made the blade flash. Deft and quick, Chef Takano carved the radish, whittling it into a rose, and presented it to Mrs. Johnson with a bow.

"Pretty," she said. "But we don't have time for this."

"Of course not," he said. "I am accustomed to having to make the best of scarce time and resources. At your service."

"Well, there are vegetables to chop for soup. If that's not too ordinary for you."

The Japanese chef's knife danced up and down a carrot, mincing it into a fine dice. Mrs. Johnson looked on with covert admiration, nodding slightly with his quick strokes as though she were keeping time.

After supper, I bicycled into town, full of self-importance. I was on a mission, a humanitarian mission. Brave and daring—like the French girl in the newscast, the Resistance girl.

Grace was giving a lesson when I arrived. Standing in her cool foyer, listening to the music, inhaling the smell of furniture polish, I felt like a girl again, waiting my turn for my lesson.

Quietly I climbed the stairs. I rummaged in my boxes of books, stored in the closet of her spare room, the room she called mine. My father had given me a book for every Christmas and birthday. Books had provided constant company, even during the lonely time when Neal seemed to forget me in high school. What should I pick for Charlotte? I selected *Tom Sawyer, Little Women, The Five Little Peppers.* American stories. I hoped she would like them.

Before leaving, I looked around the room. What else I might want to take back to the hotel with me? My eyes fell on my handwork basket. The half-finished sweater I'd started for Neal reproached me. It was too hot to think of holding yarn and knitting. I had started the sweater the previous fall. Grace helped me cast on and learn the cable stitch. Knitting the sweater had seemed a way to keep him close—magic protection. And after the notice came at Halloween, after I knew he was missing, I kept knitting. By now, it had been months since I'd touched it. I tried to push the thought away but I couldn't *see* him wearing the sweater and could not force myself to pick up the needles and the yarn again.

But I did reach in the basket to retrieve my mother's embroidery scissors—a graceful silver crane, its long gold beak formed by the blades. A gold crane for good luck, Mr. Takano had said.

"Stay the night," Grace said, coming to the door. "You look tired. They're working you too hard out there."

"I need to get back," I said, eager to complete my errand. "There's a little girl at the hotel, I'm lending her these books."

"Can she read English?"

"She's half-English," I said.

"You sweet thing," Grace said, embracing me. Her arms were cool, I inhaled her lavender scent. "Your father would like that."

Charlotte was nowhere to be seen, but I found her father on the porch. I approached Takeo Harada warily, a little shy.

"These books are for your daughter," I said.

"She doesn't need to be singled out. The nail that sticks out gets pounded in. She is conspicuous enough."

His stern expression, the rejection, shocked me. Stung, I turned away.

"But leave the books," he said.

"Here," I said, fumbling, dropping the books at his feet in my surprise.

He stooped and helped me gather them up. He looked at me, unsmiling. His eyes were black, the deepest black I had ever seen.

"Thank you," he said.

***

The next morning as I walked down the kitchen steps with my boss's breakfast tray, Mr. Takano greeted me from where he sat, sipping from a small bowl.

"Good morning," he said. "A tea break. I seem to have indigestion, little pains." With a wistful look he said, "I crave plum jam, and a cup of *gyokura*."

"A cup of what?"

"*Gyokura*, jewel tea. The best leaf tea. I miss tastes of my childhood most of all at breakfast. *Yudofu*—bean curd in broth. *Umeboshi*—pickled plums."

"Pickled plums?" Mrs. Johnson stood at the screen door, listening. "I've never pickled plums. Water melon rind, cucumbers—

not plums."

"We use only the best ones, bright yellow. Steep them twice, in *shochu* liquor, and then red *shiho* tea. We let them season, in the cool dark closet behind our futons."

"Futons?" I asked.

"Our quilts and beds, in one. We take them out at night, sleep on the floor."

"Sounds uncomfortable," Mrs. Johnson said. "Hazel, don't dawdle, get that tray up to Mr. Phelps while it's still hot. So, what is this *shochu*?"

I left the two cooks talking shop.

In the morning mail, Mr. Phelps received a resolution from a VFW chapter in Allegheny County.

Whereas: The Japanese Nationals, captured in Germany and other Axis Countries, were brought to this Country and housed at the Bedford Springs Hotel, one of the finest hotels in this country, and

Whereas: The Nationals of the United States and other Allied Countries captured by the Japanese were housed in concentration camps in the Philippines and other Countries in control of the Japanese, and placed in the same status of War Prisoners, therefore be it

Resolved by Allegheny County Council, Veterans of Foreign Wars of the United States

that we protest the pampering of these Japanese Prisoners and petition the Department of Justice that, pending their status, these Japanese Prisoners be removed from the Bedford Springs Hotel and placed in Concentration Camps.

My boss re-folded it again and stuffed it back in the envelope.

"Send this along to Under Secretary Grew at State—they listen to him. He was a prisoner of the Japanese himself," Phelps instructed me. "Dealing with the public is like stamping out molehills—satisfy one congressman, pacify a reporter, and someone else pops up."

"What about this, sir?" I asked, holding out a letter. "It's from a minister in New York."

"Who? What crackpot is going to crawl out of the woodwork next." He was exasperated today.

"No. This is someone looking for some Japanese people he knew."

He took off his glasses and rubbed the bridge of his nose. "Read it to me, Hazel."

"For many years I have been deeply interested in Japan and her people, coming to know some of the Japanese Americans through the mission work of my church. Pearl Harbor was a devastating shock to me and a blow to our hopes for our mission work. Nevertheless, the reprehensible acts of the Japanese military have not destroyed my faith in the good people I have known. I am deeply concerned to know the whereabouts and welfare of my friends Otoshiro and Meiko Kuroda and would appreciate any light you can shed on this.

If not incompatible with the public interest to do so, would you be so kind as to inform me whether, among the number said to have been brought here, there is one Otoshiro Kuroda? Mr. Kuroda's American born wife, nee Meiko Yamada, was among our dearest friends. Meiko married in our church. When Meiko's husband left this country for his post in Germany, Meiko left to wait for him in Japan. We have had no word from Otoshiro or Meiko.

Despite the war, kisuna (the bonds of friendship) endure.

Sincerely, Reverend James Nash."

"Write and tell him we have no Kuroda family here," Phelps said. "Tell him—I'm sorry."

My hands trembled as I typed, hitting each key firmly. My Underwood Noiseless was indeed a quieter machine than most, but today it seemed to clatter as though broadcasting to Mr. Phelps what I was up to.

> *I am so sorry we don't know where your friends are. But perhaps you could help our detainees, in honor of your friends. The detainees here have nothing to read. Their books were all confiscated in France. We have limited access to English language books for them, but nothing in Japanese. If through your connections with the Japanese American Society you know of anyone who would be willing to help, books would be most welcome. You could send them here, to my attention.*

> *Yours truly, Hazel Shaw*

The telephone rang as I sealed the envelope.

"We've called an ambulance," Mrs. Johnson gasped. "The Japanese cook has collapsed. Just keeled over on the floor. Tell Mr. P."

My boss flew down the hill, far ahead of me on his long legs.

The kitchen staff huddled in a corner. The ambassador's physician was trying to resuscitate Mr. Takano. He did not stop until my family doctor, Dr. Timmons, arrived from town and pronounced him dead.

Mr. Phelps met with Ambassador Oshima and Dr. Timmons in the office.

"He will be cremated. I will take the ashes to Japan," said Mr. Oshima.

"Cremation's not the custom here," said Dr. Timmons.

"Do you think it could be arranged?" Mr. Phelps asked the doctor.

"Perhaps," Dr. Timmons said, regarding me with a sad, kind expression. He had closed my father's eyes the year before; Mr. Pate from the funeral home in town had collected his body.

Things come in threes, I'd always heard. My father's death and Chef Takano's made two. Would Neal be the third?

"Get the Pates on the line, please, Hazel," said Mr. Phelps.

Mrs. Pate called back, after consulting with her husband. "Tell Mr. Phelps we'll send the remains to Pittsburgh for cremation. Barbaric practice, isn't it?"

I did not pass that last part of her message along. Not with Ambassador Oshima still in the office, glowering.

Later, everyone—staff and detainees—mingled together for once and watched from the porch as the hearse arrived.

"His wife is in Paris," I said.

"He told me," said Mrs. Johnson. "Worried they were running out of money."

"Now she won't even know he's dead," I said.

"What if they burned you and you weren't really dead?" asked Cora.

"Don't be ridiculous, Cora. The poor man is certainly dead," said Mrs. Johnson.

Charlotte Harada slipped up beside us. "When they broke my doll, in Le Havre, he gave me a special box for her. He said when we got to Japan, we would take her to a temple, for the ceremony for broken dolls. Lots of children would bring theirs, too. A priest would pray and the dolls would be burned so they could go up into the sky."

The Japanese men formed a long double line. Even Ambassador Oshima bowed as the undertakers carried the covered gurney to the car.

"Wave until he's out of sight," Charlotte said. "That's the Japanese way to say good-bye."

There was a pressure behind my eyes, the ache of unshed tears.

That night, my mother's clock ticked loudly. My room felt like an oven. I turned the pillow over and over in a futile attempt to find cool, fresh linen and finally gave up. Pinning my hair off my neck, barefoot, in my long cotton gown and robe, I sat outside on the top step, leaning against the balustrade. A shooting star dropped behind the dark bulk of Evitt's Mountain. A whippoorwill repeated its monotonous lament, over and over again. Neal used to imitate bird songs: he cupped his hands over his mouth and warbled and whistled. He called woodcocks down out of the night sky, tricked them into twirling down into a meadow.

On the landing below, someone coughed. I froze, squinted into the shadows, and discerned Takeo Harada standing at the bottom of the flight of stairs, on the landing of the balcony leading to his room. I crept down the stairs.

"I am sorry about Mr. Takano," I said softly. If I startled him, he did not show any surprise. He turned and gave a slight bow, as though it were perfectly natural to be meeting. Perhaps diplomats, especially Japanese diplomats, are so trained their manners never fail them.

"He is fortunate to be spared further shame. But to be buried here, to have to remain here, that is a hardship."

"Actually, they're making arrangements for the Ambassador to take his ashes back to Japan."

"Good."

And then we just stood, quiet. A whippoorwill called in the darkness. Mr. Harada seemed lost in thought. I was just about to slip away when he spoke.

"This is the season of Obon. We light floating lanterns in the Nagasaki bay for our ancestors, for the year's departed. To guide their spirits home."

He bowed then, and turned away toward his room.

I climbed the staircase. The image of floating lanterns stayed with me as I fell asleep: a flotilla of floating lanterns bobbing along Shober's Run across the road, guiding Neal and my father home.

***

A woman reporter was coming to visit. "Aunt Amy" wrote a very popular newspaper column in Johnstown and was somewhat of a local celebrity. I was excited when I saw her name on the approved visitor's schedule.

"Could I show her around? I was on the high school newspaper," I told Mr. Phelps.

"She's doing a human interest story," he said. "Just don't give away any state secrets."

I had expected someone much older. The slender young woman in a fashionable suit with nipped waist and broad lapels surprised me. Brisk and inquisitive, her bright eyes glittered behind tortoiseshell glasses. She even charmed my boss into permitting interviews with a few prisoners.

"No pictures, though," he said. "Leave the camera here."

I found Nejiko Suwa and Momoyo Ono sitting on the porch. Mrs. Ono, a bright and cooperative elderly woman, often translated for Phelps and had her own colorful story. Her husband had been a professor in Kyoto, and the director of a Japanese theater company; the couple came to Italy on a sabbatical to study opera. Stranded in Europe when the war began, they eventually fled Rome to gain Oshima's protection in Berlin.

"How are they treating you here?" Aunt Amy asked her.

"Our physical needs are well attended to," Mrs. Ono said. "But the restrictions on entertainment and recreation are unnecessary. I'm desperate for something to read besides newspapers—though I appreciate that we're permitted those. The worst is—no news of our families. I last heard from my mother in Kyoto more than a year ago."

Aunt Amy took rapid notes. Several barefoot children watched her, curious.

"Where are their shoes?"

"Outgrown. And, our winter clothes were impounded. If we must winter over here …"

Nejiko Suwa spoke up from where she sat nearby. The young woman spoke softly. "We're not allowed music. They took my violin."

"Is that true?" Amy asked me.

"Yes," I said, ashamed as if it were my doing.

Amy wrinkled her forehead and scribbled on her pad.

Her column appeared in *The Johnstown Observer* the next day. I read it even before putting the local papers on Mr. Phelps's breakfast tray.

JAPS NOT IN LAP OF LUXURY!

Aunt Amy heard so much about the occupation of the Bedford Springs Hotel by Jap diplomats that we decided to make a personal investigation, and believe it is high time that the rank and file of John Q. Public is given a picture that is un-prejudiced and true …

Let me tell you, no one is sitting in the lap of luxury there. The building is an old wooden structure … more or less obsolete until the Navy picked it up and used it as a training school. And if you have a boy of perhaps eighteen years of age in your home, figure the damage he does to the

*paint and walls in his room in a year, then multiply that
by five hundred. The Navy boys were not destructive, but
naturally the place received a wear and tear... No wonder
it had to be painted and cleaned before the Japs came - for
the sake of sanitation not luxury ...*

*As far as luxury goes, the children are barefoot and there is
no entertainment allowed.*

*So I say to you who try to run the business of our very
efficient State Department, let the State Department
handle this. Who are you and I to tell the Secretary of State
what to do?*

I handed the paper to Mr. Phelps. "I think you're going to like this, for a change."

He read it. "Pretty fair, all in all. Thanks for giving her a good impression. Take the afternoon off with my compliments."

"Sir," I said on impulse. "Could I take Charlotte Harada out to see Lake Caledonia?"

"She's quite a pet of yours," he sighed. "Be discreet."

"Thank you, sir. May I say, I think it is a most appropriate humanitarian gesture," I said, proud to show off my grasp of official lingo.

"You're incorrigible," he said. "And I'll confess, I have a soft spot for her too, on account of her situation. And she's my daughter's age, actually. Here's a note for the sentry."

I found Charlotte on the porch with her father. Since the piano was forbidden, Gwendolyn Harada often remained in her room most of the day, except for required roll-calls and dinner. She still made an effort to dress for dinner every evening. Without her, Charlotte and her father seemed to have drawn closer.

The girl looked up and smiled at me. "I love *Tom Sawyer*," she said.

"I'm glad."

Her father said nothing. I cleared my throat nervously as though I were asking him a favor instead of offering one.

"Sir? I'd like to invite Charlotte to go on a walk with me. There's a lake that's not far. I have permission."

"Whose?" demanded Takeo Harada. His dark eyes fixed on me, severely. "I have explained she is not to stand out."

I felt myself blushing. "We'll be discreet. Only if you approve, of course."

He stared back at me, seeming displeased. But he turned to his daughter.

"What do you think, Charlotte? Would you like to go with Hazel Shaw? You may, if you wish."

He knew my name! It pleased me. And pleased me that by coincidence or some sort of Japanese custom, he used both my names: Hazel Shaw. The traditional Quaker form of address, given name and surname, without any honorific title. The way my father used to speak.

I rushed Charlotte along as though we were escaping. We scrambled up the hill, past the Cottage, to the delivery entrance and the back guardhouse.

The guard read my note. He looked very hard at me, and at the girl, but he waved us through.

Shober's Run flashed below us—where Neal and I had played Underground Railway, John Brown, Lost Children. I wished we could really run away, that I could take Charlotte to Grace McKee. Hide her for the duration and then, after this all ended, give her a new life, a real childhood.

"We'll cross here," I said.

"But there's no bridge."

"Take off your shoes and socks." She was an indoor child, used to confinement.

Her pale, bare feet bore the mark of the straps of her too-small shoes

I led her into the water, holding my own sandals in one hand.

Across the stream, I blotted my feet dry with my socks and put my sandals back on.

"Must I wear shoes?"

"It gets rough," I warned.

"My shoes are so tight. This is better." She forged ahead, wincing a little.

The spring bubbled out of the mountainside into a semi-circular pool surrounded by rhododendrons.

"It's like a little room," she said.

"They call this the Bridal Grotto."

"I'd like to get married in some place like this," she said. "One day."

Me too, I thought, remembering how after our courthouse wedding, on our first night in the fishing cabin, Neal promised me a proper ceremony when he came home and a real honeymoon at the Springs. We'd eat steak and baked potatoes, and room service would leave breakfast by our door, just like in the movies. I remembered how Neal loved to eat. Skinny, always ravenous, he devoured apples, crunching through the core even though I warned him the seeds had poison in them, arsenic or cyanide, I'd heard. After demolishing the apple he'd pretend to gag, let his eyes roll back into his head and flop on the ground to tease me. I fell into a daydream; Neal safely home, renewing our vows here, scratching our initials on a pane in the grand hotel dining room the way brides had for years before.

Charlotte had disappeared. What if I had lost her while daydreaming? Her father had trusted me. And Mr. Phelps.

"Charlotte!" I called. She skipped back toward me from above. "Don't go out of my sight," I ordered.

We hiked up to a rough stone shelter with a mossy roof supported on four stone piers: the Magnesium Spring House. Neal and I had kissed here. I stepped inside the pavilion, cool and dark, the stone floor glistening with moisture, the layers of past and present overlapped. A fountain bubbled in one corner. I filled my cupped hand and drank. "They say it purifies the blood."

"It smells," she said. "We stayed at another spa, in Austria, after they captured us, before sending us here. The water didn't smell like that."

"Minerals are good for you," I said. "Presidents used to come here for the waters."

"Roosevelt?" she asked. "Truman?"

"No," I said. "Polk. Buchanan."

"I never heard of them," she said, dismissive.

The steep path continued, but the pebbles gave way to spongy, packed hemlock needles.

"This feels like carpet," said Charlotte. "And it smells like my mother's cedar chest." A shadow crossed her face. "We left it there. Everything still in it."

The late summer sun beat down, dust motes filled the air. Breaking into open ground, following the old logging path the hay rides used to take, we emerged into the meadow. Crickets buzzed and chirped in the tall grass beside the trail. I named the wildflowers for her: Queen Anne's lace, purple thistles, daisies, blue-fringed chicory.

"What's this?" she asked, holding up a sprig of orange and yellow.

"Butter and eggs," I said. "A wild snapdragon."

"Snap dragon?" She giggled, her grave oval face crinkled and radiant.

I split a milkweed pod and released the silky down. "They collected it, for the war effort," I told her. "They sent it to stuff army jackets."

"We slept under featherbeds, in Berlin. But it was still cold. We burned furniture to try and stay warm. Not the cedar chest. Not the piano bench. Nothing keeps you warm when you're hungry." Her smile drained; her eyes shuttered. She looked older, much older, than her thirteen years.

The walk seemed longer than when Neal and I had hiked here. We reached the lake. The shore looked overgrown, fringed with cattails, the shallowest water covered with a mosaic of algae. But beyond the algae, beyond the cattails, the water sparkled.

"May I go in?" She looked at me. In the sunlight, her gray eyes, for the first time, had glints of green. "Please?"

"Of course!"

We waded. Puffs of mud breathed up between our toes and minnows darted away. I pushed open the door to the battered green boathouse and blinked in the sudden dark, letting my eyes adjust. Inhaling the musty cool, I walked along the floating, creaking catwalk to the rack of canoes.

"Help me," I said. "But be careful—this wood is rotten in spots."

Charlotte struggled; the boat slipped out of her grasp and splashed into the water. I dropped in paddles, a life ring, and clambered in.

The canoe lurched and shimmied; Charlotte almost tipped us over. Pushing free of the dock and out into the sunshine, I paddled along the shore, startling redwing blackbirds and a heron in the reeds.

"Cranes are sacred in Japan, my father says. They never disturb the water, taking off or landing. When I was little, I used to divide up birds into countries. Cranes are Japanese, quiet, like my father. Ducks are English, quacking, like Mama."

"Chef Takano told me he used to fold gold paper cranes, for

good luck," I said.

"I wish he hadn't died. He was nice to my father. Now how will I know when the ceremony is for the broken dolls?"

A fish jumped and splashed farther out, a turtle sculled along the surface. Dragonflies skimmed by. I tethered the boat to the floating deck in the middle of the lake and we climbed up the slippery rungs of the ladder and lay on the warm, weathered planks.

I hadn't planned to swim, but the water was irresistible. Stripped to panties and bra, I mounted the diving tower and splashed down.

"I want to try it too!" she said, shyly taking off her skirt and blouse.

She climbed and jumped, climbed and jumped, laughing like a child. That day marked the first and only time I heard her laugh out loud.

After our swim, we sat together in the sun, dangling our feet, letting our underthings dry on us. The girl chattered; I had never seen her so animated, so at ease. Among the others at the hotel, she always looked wary, watchful. Not now, here alone with me.

"I haven't been swimming in ages. They closed the baths in Berlin," she said. "And my school. Everything."

"It must have been hard," I said.

"Boring, doing only what you can do in a flat. Read. Read. Read. Practice. Practice. Practice. I'm not good on the piano like my mother. At first they let me go out in the neighborhood. I collected shrapnel. But it got too dangerous. Before the war though, my father used to take us for walks. Not in wild forests like America, but the parks have—had—woods, in Berlin. And castles! My favorite was Grunewald. My mother's favorite was Pfaueninsel, Peacock Island— because someone English planned it. My mother said English gardens are the most beautiful. He said Japanese. They used to like to argue and tease about what was best—the English way, or the Japanese. Even the moon. My mother says there is a man in the moon, he says it's a rabbit. Now she hates Japan."

The spotted shadow of a big fish passed in the water beneath us, like a ghost through the depths.

Charlotte shivered. "My father says in Japan there are giant carp, a hundred years old. He says he'll take me to see them, one day. I had a cat. It went out one night and never came back. Maybe a bomb got it. We kept a bucket of sand in the bathtub, in case of a bomb but one little bucket of sand can't keep you safe. The Zoologischer Garten was bombed. It's terrible—the smell of dead things."

I remembered her mother saying she had tried to keep Charlotte from seeing the devastation as they left Berlin. She could not keep her from smelling it.

"And the worst noise in the world is how quiet the air is just after a bomb screams but before it hits—we could even hear it get quiet when we were hiding in the cellar."

Just then, as though summoned by her description, I heard the shrill racket of sirens. The coincidence seemed eerie, ominous. Perhaps unconsciously, she'd heard the warning before she spoke. Perhaps she'd been so sensitized to listening for approaching danger that she picked up the frequency of the siren call before it was audible to me—the way dogs detect the silent summons of a whistle imperceptible to the human ear.

Then I smelled the smoke. "Hurry!" I called out.

She was already far ahead of me, tearing down the hill.

Chapter Five

From the Bridal Grotto I saw the fire engine streaking up the drive to the hotel. A blaze crackled on the front lawn. The dry summer grass burned like tinder in front of the main building, flames lapping toward the hotel.

Charlotte and I splashed across the creek.

The sentry hurried us through the front gate, calling out over the clamor of the sirens, the shouts of the firemen. "Out of the way! Get over there!"

The detainees and the staff stood clustered together beside the curving brick wall of the pool wing, watching as the firemen sprung into action, waving canvas hoses. Maintenance men and guards staggered across the lawn, lugging buckets, trying to douse the flames. The smoke was thick and acrid. My eyes streamed and I began to cough. I had lost sight of Charlotte.

A guard called roll through the megaphone, bellowing names. "Assada, Mitsuko! Assada, Kimi! Doi, Tatsu!"

Where was Charlotte? I saw Gwendolyn Harada searching the crowd, and out of the chaos, Charlotte appeared, bolting toward her mother.

A woman was screaming. Mia had broken out of the crowd, running straight at the flames. Joe blocked her flight and dragged her back to her mother.

He came and stood beside me, holding his wrist. "That crazy brat bit me. Broke the skin."

"You should ask the Ambassador's doctor to take a look at it."

"I'd rather take my chances," he said.

I ignored his slur against the Japanese doctor.

"How did it start?" I asked him.

"No telling. Arson, maybe."

Even after the firemen managed to extinguish the flames on the main lawn, a cloud of heavy smoke hung in the air with the out-of-season smell of bonfire. Later, in the office, Mr. Phelps met with the sheriff and the fire chief.

"Definitely arson. Someone's trying to burn the place down," said the Sheriff. "Someone wants to smoke them out."

"There were threats like that, at that first meeting," said my boss, sober and worried.

"I can't rule out the possibility it was an accident," said the fire chief. "You sell tobacco and cigarettes, in the commissary, right?" he asked.

"Yes," said Mr. Phelps.

"Suspend that right away. Whether someone is careless by accident, or on purpose, makes no difference if a place goes up in smoke."

"I still say arson," said the Sheriff emphatically. "People out there hate them. People in here hate us."

Several days after the fire, two brown cartons arrived from Reverend Nash in New York City, addressed to my attention. Joe ferried them up the hill in the wheelbarrow and deposited them on the floor of my office. I cut the twine on the first carton and found a note.

I hope these books bring some comfort; I send these from my personal collection of Japanese literature, in honor of my friends, the Kurodas.

"What's this?" Mr. Phelps peered over my shoulder.

"That minister in New York who wanted to find his Japanese friends? He's sent these," I said, trying to sound offhand.

"He just happened to send Japanese books," said my boss skeptically.

"I might have mentioned that they had nothing to read."

"Hazel, there's a chain of command here. By disregarding it you put everyone, everyone, in jeopardy. Fires are dangerous—but so is cavalierly disregarding authority."

"I'm sorry, sir," I said. *If you are doing the right thing, ask forgiveness not permission,* my father would say. *Obey the higher authority.*

My boss surprised me then by hitching up the knees of his carefully creased trousers, crouching beside me, and opening a volume. He ran his finger over the page. The paper looked almost like rough fabric, covered with columns of characters. A sheet of translucent tissue protected a photograph on the next page, a picture of a garden.

Mr. Phelps gave a soft whistle of admiration. "These are the real article. You win. Put them in the lounge. We are running a detainment center not a penal colony, after all."

Joe pushed the wheelbarrow up the steep path and re-loaded it with the cartons. I walked beside him as he trundled the cargo back down to the hotel.

"Opening a library?" he said.

"Might be," I said.

Charlotte appeared as we unloaded the wheelbarrow and carried the last boxes into the lounge.

"What's this?" she asked.

"Books, Japanese books!" I said.

"Have fun, ladies." Joe looked back, grinning, as he left the room.

"Is he your boyfriend?"

"No," I said. "I'm married."

"Married? Are you old enough? Where's your husband?"

"Overseas. Do you want to help me?" I was eager to forestall any more questions.

We worked side by side, unloading the books, arranging them on the shelves. The tall bookshelves in the lounge had glass doors. Before the war, the cases displayed the hotel's famous collection of local history and maps—all locked away in storage now.

"Can you tell me what these books are?" It tantalized me, and frustrated me, too.

"I can't read very much Japanese at all," said Charlotte. "Kanji are very hard to learn. And there are hundreds and hundreds. My father taught me some, but my mother doesn't like him to. May I bring him to see these books? He can tell you all about them."

"Yes," I said.

While she was gone, I arranged the last of the books on the shelves, hoping Mr. Harada would be pleased.

"See, Papa?" Charlotte danced over to the shelf. "Lots and lots of Japanese books! Hazel got them for us."

Takeo Harada withdrew a volume, opening it with care. "Basho," he said. "One of our finest poets." He looked up at me. His eyes were gleaming like some precious foreign stone. "Where did these come from? The Embassy?"

"A man in New York. A minister. He wrote to us, trying to find a Japanese friend who worked in the Embassy in Berlin," I said.

"Who was he looking for?"

"Someone named Kuroda."

"Kuroda? I knew him. He was killed in the bombing." Takeo

shook his head, and turned back to the book, gently touching the pages as he turned them. "Cha-chan" he said. "Come, read with me."

I listened, to the alternating murmur of English and Japanese as they knelt side by side on the floor. Never before had I seen a grown man kneel for such a long time. He seemed more at ease.

"Translate, Cha-chan"

"It's too hard."

"Try."

"All soldiers leave behind is grass?"

"Almost. Very good."

I listened as he continued, half-reading, half-reciting.

My father knew reams of poetry. Walt Whitman, Emily Dickinson, James Whitcomb Riley were his favorites. He used to recite to me, at bedtime, before I could read. Even after I learned to read, I loved the sound of his voice and the time together just before the day ended.

"Oh, this poem is Murasaki Shikibu's loveliest." Takeo Harada recited, slowly, in Japanese. "Cha-chan? Try again. Say it with me in Japanese first." He pointed at each character, running his finger down the page.

She joined in, hesitantly. Once or twice he corrected her. I couldn't understand them, but the sound of their combined voices, hers faint, his deep—like light and shadow—was as pleasant as music.

"Translate now."

"Why did you, did you disappear?"

"Good, go on."

"Why did you disappear into the sky? Even snow falls in the world."

"Even the delicate snow falls," he corrected. "Even the delicate snow falls in the world." Takeo Harada looked up at me, not smiling, but his expression was more open, less guarded. "She wrote it for her daughter, who had died," he said. He closed the book, gently, with care. "May I borrow this?" he asked me.

"Yes. Are all the books poetry?"

He examined them, volume by volume. "All poetry," he said. He bowed and left the room.

I walked back to my office, silently repeating that last poem. It was mysterious, sad. It spoke to me, somehow. Takeo Harada, too, would lose his daughter, if his wife's request were granted. My father told a story about two women. Both claimed the same baby. The king threatened to settle their dispute by cutting the baby in half. The true mother surrendered her claim—in order to leave the baby whole.

Ada called the office from the main switchboard later that afternoon. "It's the War Department! Something's going on."

Mr. Phelps gripped the receiver as though frozen to it as he listened. His jaw clenched and unclenched. "Yes, sir. We'll set up, right away."

He slammed down the phone and then called down to the guard station. "I want the visitors assembled right away in the dining room. The radio set up to broadcast. Translators. Now! The President is making an announcement."

I ran down the hill toward the main building. The gong from the lobby clanged and bonged and then the siren pealed. It felt like another emergency.

"Everyone to the dining room!" a guard bellowed through the megaphone.

The prisoners filed into the dining room, followed by the guards and all the staff. I leaned against the back wall, near the girls from the kitchen. A radio had been set up on a podium at the end of the room. It crackled with static, and then the announcer said "Stand by, stand by."

President Truman's voice startled me. Somehow, when someone said "The President" I still expected the familiar tones of Roosevelt, the voice that used to fill our living room, the voice my father used to talk back to familiarly. I wanted it to be Roosevelt's voice. I wanted my father to be here.

> *"Sixteen hours ago, an American airplane dropped one bomb on the Japanese city of Hiroshima and destroyed its usefulness to the enemy. That bomb had more power than 20,000 pounds of TNT. It is an atomic bomb. It is a harnessing of the basic power of the universe. The force from which the sun draws its power has been loosed against those who brought war to the Far East. We have spent two billion dollars on the greatest scientific gamble in history and won.*
>
> *We are now prepared to obliterate more rapidly and completely every productive enterprise the Japanese have above ground in any city. We shall destroy their docks, their factories, and their communications. Let there be no mistake; we shall completely destroy Japan's power to make war. If they do not now accept our terms they may expect a rain of ruin from the air the like of which has never been seen on earth."*

Rain of ruin. The words chilled, like the weird shadow of the long-ago solar eclipse. My father and I had walked to the park by the Juniata; in the middle of the hot mid-day, the sun darkened and the birds stopped singing. Now, I felt the same dread—as though we were all threatened by a rain of ruin, not just Japan, thousands of miles away. *No man is an island,* my father said. I saw in my mind's eye the archipelago of islands in the Leyte Gulf where Neal had disappeared.

Mrs. Ono interpreted, after the President finished and the announcer signed off. The room fell into dead silence.

The children played after dinner as though it were any other night. The older ones dared to venture beyond the burnt lawn into the unspoiled grass beyond the pool wing. Their sand pile had been used up, putting out the fire. Shadows stretched across the lawn as they raced through the blue evening, back and forth, chattering and laughing like birds, catching fireflies and releasing them to fly upward like lazy sparks. For once, the mothers let them stay up late. No one wanted to be upstairs, alone, in the dark. Finally, the floodlights along the perimeter beyond the fence blazed on, bleaching the purple evening to gray, and the curfew siren sounded early.

Joe found me. "Hazel," he said. "I'm going into town. Have to get out of here for a breath of fresh air. Come with me."

"I don't think so," I said, feeling somehow anxious about leaving the hotel. As though something terrible might happen to it, to everyone here, while we were gone. It seemed safer here. After all, there were arsonists out there. I couldn't keep track any more of who was the enemy.

"Come on," he said. "It's no good brooding. I have to take a car for a run anyway." The absentee hotel owner, Mr. Gardner, had left instructions to keep the cars well-maintained. Joe tuned them up and washed and polished them, and drove them in rotation—not far, not wasting precious gas, but just enough, he said, to make sure they were running smoothly.

"There's a new picture at the Pitt," he persisted. "Frank Sinatra and Gene Kelly."

"Okay," I said, relenting. If anything could distract me from the sense of dread and the shadow that hung over the day, it would be Gene Kelly.

We drove into the square, each corner secured by a familiar building: Post Office, Courthouse, Lutheran Church, Presbyterian. Lawyers Row was dark, except for one window, someone working late. The granite Union soldier on the Civil War Monument stood guard over the square, looking like a giant chess piece, my father used to say. Everything was the same. Everything was still here.

The poster by the ticket booth announced: *ANCHORS AWEIGH, with Frank Sinatra and Gene Kelly!*

Joe paid for our tickets.

"How is it out there at the Springs?" asked the usher. "How'd the Japs take the news?"

"No fuss," said Joe. "Quiet."

The theater was a cavernous space, with a painted ceiling of cherubs and clouds—stained and chipping from the leaks above. Joe stumbled a bit on the steep aisle. I chose my favorite seats—middle of the center row—and settled in as the dusty red velvet curtain rattled open.

General MacArthur filled the screen. The quiet air in the auditorium felt thick and ominous.

A cadaverous man stepped out of a bamboo cage and shook the General's hand, and looked out at me, with the haunted eyes of a dying animal.

The narrator's voice jerked and skipped: "Captured by the Japanese in the Philippines, liberated by American forces. These men survived months of starvation, of torture if they didn't bow at the correct angle."

Just before you fall through ice you sense disaster; you anticipate the solid surface giving way. Then it splinters and the cracks shoot out beneath your feet, and the chasm opens. Perhaps I trembled, or even cried out.

Joe put his arm around my shoulder. "Are you all right?" he

whispered.

I fled up the aisle into the fading summer evening light.

"Wait!" Joe called after me, but I couldn't wait and, with his bad leg, he couldn't catch me.

Racing down the street, I passed the hardware store, the jewelry shop where Neal bought my engagement ring. In the park by the river, I sat on a swing in the rusty, neglected playground, gulping in deep breaths of damp evening air, inhaling the velvety scent of the Juniata River. Two boys fished in waders beneath the bridge, just where my father had taught me how to cast, and to skip stones if the fish weren't biting.

Sometimes on weekends, when we were in grade school, Neal and I used to race from the Jail down to the river playground. He outran me, with his long legs. I panted behind, watching the soles of his shoes flash up and down. We'd rest on the swings, and I'd pump hard as I could, trying to send the swing over the bar on the swing set (mythical, impossible goal). He'd swing, too, folding his long legs beneath him so they wouldn't drag on the ground and slow him down. At the top of the arc, I'd shout out the count: "ONE! TWO! THREE!" and we'd both let go, launching ourselves into the sky, landing on the hard-packed earth. We would lie there, looking up at the swirling sky as we caught our breath.

Now, I sat on the swing, twisting to tangle the chains. I let them unwind; I pumped, hard, hurtling up, swooping down. And jumped, deliberately landing hard, jarring back to ground. Brushing myself off, I got to my feet. Joe was leaning against the back of the bench, catching his breath. I sat on the bench and he came and sat beside me. We watched the river, the clouds of gnats. The last light was fading.

"I just wanted to distract you. Instead—oh, God, Hazel, I rub your face in it. I'm really sorry."

"Not your fault. It's there, all the time, you know? Let's go back to the hotel."

Why did you disappear into the sky? I chanted the Japanese poet's words to myself, over and over, all the way back to the hotel.

Two days later we all gathered in the dining room again, summoned by Mr. Phelps to hear President Truman. The President's thin, disembodied voice celebrated another success. Another atom bomb had been dropped. On Nagasaki. His warning seemed directed right at us:

> *"If Japan does not surrender, bombs will have to be dropped on her war industries and, unfortunately, thousands of civilian lives will be lost. I urge Japanese civilians to leave industrial cities immediately, and save themselves from destruction."*

Ambassador Oshima listened with his chin jutting at its usual pugnacious angle, surrounded by his retinue of attachés. No one flinched. But I heard muffled sobbing and discovered Gwendolyn Harada weeping just behind me. Charlotte hugged her mother's waist, buried her head in her mother's skirt. Takeo Harada stood across the room beside the windows, his back to the crowd. He stood very straight, still as a statue, facing the darkening sky. I thought of his description of the Nagasaki bay, alight with lanterns. Alight with beacons for the dead.

As the crowd dispersed, Charlotte caught my elbow, pulling me to a halt.

"Ask Mr. Phelps to contact my grandparents."

"He's trying," I said. "He's talked to the British Embassy in Washington."

"My other grandparents. In Nagasaki."

"I'll ask," I said. But I knew her Harada grandparents were out of reach, beyond the longest strings that could be pulled. I knew that, even before reading the next morning's headline in the *Gazette:* "Nagasaki Crushed by Blast Too Terrible to Believe."

I hadn't been to Meeting in all the weeks at the hotel, but I needed to go that Sunday. Mr. Phelps said Joe could drive me out to Dunning's Creek.

The Meeting House was full, full as it had been when my father was buried. Joe and I squeezed in on a bench near the door. I sank into the silence in the room. What might my father say if he were here? But I couldn't hear him. I couldn't even remember his voice.

The heat released the aromatic scent of cedar from the heavy rafters. Through the old bubbled glass windows I watched clouds scud by outside. *Why did you disappear into the sky?* The line of poetry had lodged in my brain.

No one spoke for the whole hour, but the full communal silence somehow comforted me.

Meeting ended; the elders on the facing bench shook hands. I turned to Joe, holding out my hand. He hesitated, wrinkling his brow. "It's just the way we finish," I reminded him.

The Clerk stood. She was a tiny woman, with a shock of short white hair. Before she retired, she had been a nurse. My father said she had been there the day I was born and my mother died.

"Good morning, Friends. Please, if you know of those among us to be held in the Light," said the Clerk.

This was the moment in Meeting to request prayers on behalf of the ill, the grieving.

I stood, gripping the back of the bench in front of me.

"There are Japanese children among us, at the Springs. Only a few read English—but if you have any picture books. And if you have any paper, colored pencils ... could you bring them to the hotel, please?"

I expected Joe to say something critical when I sat down again.

But he didn't. I looked at him, and he looked at me—and nodded.

Afterward, as we walked outside, the Clerk found me. "We've missed thee, Hazel," she said. "Thank you for your message. We have what thee seeks for the children, in the First Day classroom. Come with me."

And so Joe and I drove back to the Springs with the Meeting's school supplies—paper, pencils, and colored pencils, boxes of watercolors. I arranged the art materials on a low shelf in my library. Without even consulting Mr. Phelps (ask forgiveness, not permission) I made an announcement that evening at dinner.

"There are art supplies for the children in the lounge. A gift from the Friends Meeting. Please, if you like, come take some." By curfew, the shelf was bare.

Chapter Six

An avalanche of news, mail, and cables arrived, covering the office in untidy stacks. A steady stream of detainees requested appointments: since the bombs, anyone with a tie to the West—a French or German spouse left behind, or young adult Japanese born in Europe—sought special dispensation to avoid being sent to Japan.

Mr. Phelps heard each request, and dictated the promised letters of inquiry to Secretary Acheson—an exercise in futility, he told me, since none would be granted. "A matter of precedent. Grant one, have to grant all."

"Not even Gwendolyn Harada? Charlotte?"

"She's no exception." He shot me a warning look. "No partiality."

"I just wondered." I did not know what to hope for, what to wish for Charlotte and her family. I kept thinking of that king, a baby cut in two.

I had never asked Phelps to try and find Charlotte's paternal grandparents in Nagasaki. The somber backdrop of the partial, slowly unfolding news of the bombs' aftermath answered the unasked question.

Daily life continued. A dentist visited from town to take care of urgencies among the visitors, setting up a temporary clinic in one corner of the ballroom upstairs. The State Department authorized detainees to withdraw additional funds from their accounts. Even so, with rationing, shoes proved unobtainable, and warm clothing scarce. Hand-me-downs arrived from the Meeting—without my even requesting them.

Mr. Phelps returned Gwendolyn Harada's music and Nejiko Suwa's violin.

"We all need consolation," he said to me.

The two women played again in the evenings in the lounge to a small audience. My boss hovered beside the door. Takeo Harada listened from an armchair in the corner; he seemed deeply weary, detached.

My library's shelves emptied as books passed from hand to hand; the Japanese greeted me with bows when I encountered them on the grounds or in the hotel. Once they had all looked alike to me, and I suppose to them I had been one indistinguishable American girl among many. The books and the art supplies differentiated me.

But if the books enhanced my standing with the detainees, Mrs. Johnson grew stricter and reprimanded me for tardiness, for being careless in returning dishes from the Cottage office to the kitchen. And when I paused on Cora's threshold, the gossiping girls fell silent.

"I'm sorry, Hazel," she said when we encountered each other at bedtime beside the bathroom door. "It's just—not everyone understands what you're doing."

She tried to hug me, apologetic, but I brushed her off.

The implied criticisms provoked me. I was lonely.

I persuaded Joe to take me to town to borrow books from the library for Charlotte. He helped me carry the books to the car. The librarian let me have many more than the usual quota of four. I also borrowed from the poetry shelf in the adult section—Whitman and

Dickinson, my father's favorites. Takeo Harada might like them.

"Who's all this poetry for?" Joe asked, with a touch of suspicion.

"Me."

He drove faster than usual back along the narrow road to the hotel, swerving around the curves. Again uneasiness muddled the air between us.

I found Charlotte and gave her an armload of new books.

"Oh—more Louisa May Alcott! I love her."

"And I've brought some poetry, for your father."

She rubbed the tip of her nose with her forefinger, nibbled the fingernail. "I don't know —he's not reading, or doing anything really, these days. He's sad, Hazel."

"Just give them to him, please." I had marked a page in the Dickinson for him—about there being a certain slant of light on winter afternoons, about shadows holding their breath. It reminded me of the Japanese poem about disappearing into the sky.

I lay awake for hours every night now and was so tired I sleep-walked through the days. I had no energy for ping pong with Joe in the evenings. At least Mr. Phelps had permitted Mrs. Harada and Nejiko to start playing again. The best moment all day was listening to them. Later, after the detainees' curfew, I swam in the indoor pool—longer every night, to tire myself out. I would unlock the door and slip into the water without turning on any lights— the band of clerestory windows admitted enough light from the spotlights outside. I liked swimming alone in the dimness, in the soft mineral water.

Wednesday, the fourteenth of August, my boss asked me to come back to the office after dinner. "I need you," he said, looking very solemn.

Another bomb, I thought. Another bomb. What will be left over there?

The phone was already ringing when I reached my desk. It was

Ada from the lobby switchboard.

"Call from Washington for him," she said.

He closed the connecting door between our offices and took the call from Secretary Byrnes.

Afterward, he came and sat on the corner of my desk. He took off his glasses, rubbed his eyes, and bowed his head. And then he looked up. Without his glasses, he looked very tired. "It's over, Hazel."

"Over?"

"They have surrendered."

I looked down at the hotel. The lights were still on in the kitchen for the after-supper dishes, as though it were any evening. It was over. All of this would end soon, too. All of them would go. Our small world was about to disappear like morning mist burning off the river.

Once again, Mr. Phelps ordered everyone to assemble for a broadcast. Everyone surely expected news of another bomb. The room was so quiet. It was a full quiet, like the quiet in the Meeting House, but full of sadness.

Mr. Phelps directed his remarks to Ambassador Oshima. "I have the honor to inform you, sir, that President Truman has received a note of total capitulation from your Emperor, full acceptance of the Potsdam Declaration, containing no qualifications."

The Ambassador's heavy head jerked very, very slightly. Regaining his composure, he nodded curtly and ordered Mrs. Ono to interpret.

Lytton Phelps continued. "The formal signing of the peace will occur at the earliest possible moment. Armistice conditions prevail. We hope a bloodless surrender may be effectuated. The President and Secretary of State assure your safety, rights, and well-being, like that of all prisoners of war and civilian internees, will be scrupulously preserved."

A cacophony outside drowned him out: the roar of approaching cars, a clamor of horns honking. An angry victory parade was streaming into the narrow valley, converging toward the hotel.

The guards shouted through megaphones and ordered the detainees to their rooms.

Everyone dispersed quickly, in absolute quiet except for a few weeping, frightened children held tightly in their mothers' arms. Takeo Harada passed within inches of me, walking blindly, mechanically, eyes fixed straight ahead.

A group of revelers stood at the gate to the hotel beside the guard box, chanting, "Nips go home! Nips go home!"

"What will happen if they get in?" I asked Joe. "Should everyone—hide?"

"The guards will keep it under control." Surprising me, he grabbed my shoulders and spun me around. "There's nothing to be afraid of anymore! This is it! VJ Day!" He kissed me on the forehead. I pulled away. Cora was standing beside me and Joe twirled her around next, as though we were at a festive square dance, changing partners.

The shouting from the road beyond the wall grew louder. The guards forced the boisterous crowd away from the gate, but they didn't leave. It was like a siege.

"I need you back in the office." Mr. Phelps said. I was grateful to be busy.

Ada forwarded calls all evening—from Washington, the press.

Close to midnight, Mrs. Johnson, dressed in her best black dress with a lace collar, arrived with a silver tray and a bottle of wine in an ice bucket. "Champagne from the hotel cellar, with Mr. Gardner's compliments." The absentee owner managed another hotel, The Shoreham in Washington. I'd never met him. Mrs. Johnson said he'd retire and come here full time as soon as the war ended. She looked forward to that.

"Stay and join us, Prudence."

"Thank you, sir, I will. We did it, sir!"

"Yes. We did."

Phelps popped the cork with a hollow retort, like a gun shot. He poured three glasses from the glistening dark green bottle. "To victory," he said. "To peace."

"And getting things back to normal," said Mrs. Johnson. She smiled, not her usual prim, buttoned-up smile, but a broad smile. They clinked glasses and turned to me.

I clinked and sipped, not sure what to wish for. The bubbles stung my tongue.

The next morning, Gwendolyn Harada came to the office without an appointment.

She looked pale, dark circles under her eyes.

"You haven't—heard anything—about me?" she whispered.

I shook my head.

"You sent the letters?"

I nodded, looking over my shoulder, nervous that my boss would overhear.

"Please," she said. "I must speak to him."

"You need an appointment."

She marched past my desk and into his office.

"What does this mean for me?" she asked him. "And my daughter?"

"No change to your status. You remain a diplomatic detainee. However, since prisoner exchange is now irrelevant, expect orders for repatriation soon. Just a matter of availability of transport to the West Coast and then Japan."

"But it's not repatriation for me. What does my Embassy say?"

"Nothing, Mrs. Harada."

The letter I had smuggled made no difference. I had felt so brave and powerful.

"Please, let me speak with my ambassador directly." Her voice broke.

He capitulated. "Very well," he said. "Have Ada connect us!" he called out to me.

After Ada put the call through, Mr. Phelps came out of his office and shut the pocket doors. "Let's give her some privacy," he said. I don't know if it was what Mrs. Harada said, or just the circumstances. Maybe more punishment seemed pointless to the officials, too, now that we were at peace. Or maybe the officials wanted to punish Takeo Harada more and knew this was the way? Or perhaps it had been decided beforehand, just tied up in red tape. However it came about, by week's end, the order arrived from the British Embassy:

Re: Gwendolyn Mason Harada. Since the aforementioned served in no official capacity for the government of Japan, it has been decided to permit her to have her British status and rights reinstated, and to permit her return immediately, with her minor child—providing the father permits. Mrs. Harada is to be remanded to Washington, to the Embassy, immediately.

Lytton Phelps sent me to find Takeo and Gwendolyn Harada, and bring them to the Cottage. I followed behind the couple as they walked up the hill together. Almost the same height, shoulder to shoulder, copper and ebony hair glinting in the sun, they walked without touching. But they were perfectly in step, like separated dance partners hearing the same music.

My boss shifted in his chair, looking back and forth between them. "Mrs. Harada, you and your daughter have been called to Washington. And will be sent to Britain."

Gwendolyn Harada let out a small gasp.

"Very well," her husband said. His voice was calm and flat.

She touched his arm. "Thank you."

"And on the matter of my wife's request for a divorce?"

"Mrs. Harada has not established sufficient residency."

"Takeo," she said softly, "That's just as well, isn't it? Perhaps,

perhaps I acted hastily, I've been so afraid. Perhaps—we might find a way, eventually. Later, you could join us there."

He ignored her, shook her hand away. "When will they depart?"

"The Embassy is sending a car, tomorrow."

"May we speak with our daughter in private? Here?" Takeo Harada fixed Mr. Phelps with an unblinking stare. It was an order, not a request.

"Of course. Hazel, please fetch Charlotte."

I found her reading on the porch. "My parents are up there, with him," she said.

"Yes," I said. "They want to talk to you."

She didn't ask for any explanation. I believe she knew. She only betrayed her worry by walking fast, ahead of me. The girl had grown taller over the weeks here; her pleated skirt swung several inches above the delicate tendons behind her knees. She had her parents' perfect posture—a diplomat's daughter, a performer's daughter.

Phelps and I waited on the Cottage porch while the family talked inside.

"Lousy situation for all of them. But this is best for the kid," he said. "Japan's a disaster, and never was any place for a foreign woman."

"Couldn't they all just stay here?"

"Ah, Hazel," he said. "I'll miss you. You're such a dreamer."

The screen door burst open. Charlotte leapt down the porch steps and lunged downhill.

"Charlotte!" Her mother called out after her, but did not follow.

Takeo Harada bowed to Phelps and then descended, at a measured, stately pace, to the hotel.

Gwendolyn Harada collapsed on the porch steps and bowed her head. She wept—deep, groaning sobs.

"It's for the best, ma'am," said Mr. Phelps, leaning down and touching her shoulder gently.

After dinner, Gwendolyn Harada and Nejiko Suwa played together for the last time. The English woman seemed perfectly composed. Finally, the younger woman put down her bow. "Play some Chopin, Gwendolyn," said Nejiko Suwa. Mrs. Harada played on alone.

I glimpsed Takeo Harada, standing outside the French doors on the porch, almost hidden. The way he stood there, watching her but erasing himself from the scene, made me shiver.

After curfew, I swam a long time. You can't cry underwater, I'd discovered.

The siren sounded before breakfast.

"What is it?" I asked Joe, running into the lobby.

"That English girl, she's disappeared. Run away, they think. And that crazy little one is gone, too. Mia."

Phelps ordered the guards to search the hotel grounds and outbuildings.

Gwendolyn Harada stalked up and down the porch, staring out at the mountainside beyond the fence.

Mia's mother Keiko Mitsuno sat in a rocking chair, face in her hands. Takeo Harada waited as though at attention, straight and still as the pillar beside him.

And then Charlotte appeared, streaking across the lawn. "Mia's in the pool! Help!"

My blood ran cold. Ever since, I've known it's not a figure of speech. Cold to the bone, reeling with shock and guilt, I ran with them toward the pool. It was my fault. I must have left the door open.

By the time I arrived, one of the guards had pulled her out and was trying to resuscitate her. Keiko Mitsuno flew across the tile floor and knelt beside her daughter, as pale as the girl. Gwendolyn Harada held Charlotte back, shielding her. The girl trembled and struggled in her mother's arms, shivering in drenched clothing. "I tried to get her out," she said. "To pull her out ... I jumped in."

Breathe, I willed Mia, breathe. Unable to watch, I fixed my eyes on the intricate basket-weave of the tile floor. Had I forgotten to lock the door the night before? If she died, I was to blame.

Dr. Doi, the Ambassador's doctor, hurried in—wearing cotton pajamas, barefoot, dark hair sticking up in unruly tufts. He pushed the guard aside and crouched beside the girl, taking her pulse, opening her eyes.

"She's gone," he said.

Keiko Mitsuno stretched out on the cold tile floor beside her child.

"How did you get in here?" Lytton Phelps asked Charlotte, gently.

"The door was open. I just wanted a place to hide. I didn't know she followed me."

Joe broke in. "Sir, I cleaned the drains early this morning. It's my fault. I must have forgotten to lock up."

For a moment, I felt overcome with relief. But—Joe knew my habits, and I knew his. He would never work before breakfast. Joe knew I'd been swimming.

I let the moment, the moment I should have spoken, pass.

"Careless, and tragic," my boss said sternly. "I am disappointed in you, Joe."

The hearse arrived for Mia. The undertaker, Mr. Pate, and his sons loaded the small gurney and shut the back hatch. Mia's mother pounded on the hearse, Takeo Harada gently pulled her away.

Joe and I walked back alone.

"You didn't clean the drains this morning."

"Says who? Anyway, they broke the rules. No reason for you to take the blame for the girls trespassing."

"But it was my fault."

He said nothing. His promise to Neal hung between us.

"Joe, you don't have to protect me."

"I cleaned the drains this morning."

"I can take care of myself."

"Could have fooled me," he said, hunching his shoulders and thrust his hands into his pants pockets. Fatigue, or anger, accentuated the limp.

That night, I had the dream for the first time. Gasping, struggling, drowning myself, I tried to rescue a child. I pulled her heavy body to the surface of the water; she slipped out of my grasp and floated down. I awoke sweaty, tangled in the sheets—with a sickening sense of guilt. And couldn't reassure myself, couldn't tell myself that it was just a dream.

Chapter Seven

Not long after the hearse left, the rain began. Another black car pulled up the drive—not a hearse this time, but the limousine from the British Embassy.

I saw it arrive, from my room up under the eaves. Unmistakable, what it was, and who it had come for. The pearls—I had to give Gwendolyn Harada her necklace. I opened the drawer and dropped the satin jewelry pouch in my pocket. The embroidery scissors, my mother's bird scissors, lay on the dresser scarf. I scooped them up, too: bird scissors, crane scissors for Charlotte.

Gwendolyn Harada stood by the porch railing, wearing the suit she'd arrived in, and the hat, and her only shoes—the brave, scuffed spectator pumps.

"Good-bye," I said, approaching her. I stood very close, so no one could see. I opened my hand, revealing the jewelry pouch. She stared so hard that for a moment I was certain she would take it. Her lips tightened and she shook her head, stepping back a pace.

Charlotte ran up to us, dressed like an English schoolgirl in her too-short gray pleated skirt and blue blouse with a scalloped white collar. But I had never seen her look more Japanese, more like her father. Her features were sharper than his, but there was the same still resignation. Her face did not look like a child's today.

"I left the books in my room for you," she said.

"You could have kept mine."

"They'd only take them away from me."

"I brought something for you," I said.

Her mother looked at me sharply.

"Bird scissors," I said.

"A heron," Charlotte said, delighted. "They're small. I'll hide them so no one can take them."

I began to cry.

"My father says, the eyes of a daughter of the samurai must never be wet," she said. "Don't cry. You can't see me if you cry. Wave when I go," she said—suddenly fierce. "Wave till I am out of sight. The Japanese way."

She hugged me then, hard and impetuously. I held her. She felt small in my arms, like a bird. And then she ran to her father. She stood facing him, looking up. He rested his hands on her shoulders, all the while looking across at his wife. Mrs. Harada stared fixedly at the black car below.

The embassy chauffeur walked up the steps beneath a giant black umbrella.

"It's time, Charlotte," she said, looking at her husband as she spoke.

Mr. Harada lifted his hands from Charlotte's shoulders and gently turned her toward her mother.

"Papa!" said the girl, spinning back to face him.

"It is time," he said, folding his arms across his chest and stepping out of reach.

The chauffeur held the umbrella up.

"This way, ladies."

The limousine pulled away. A small white hand waved through the back window. The blinking red tail lights receded down the drive.

I waved, even after the car passed the sentry and turned onto Route 220. I waved them out of sight. Takeo Harada did not wave.

The rain drummed down all morning. The hotel filled with damp cold air.

After lunch, I went to the room Charlotte and her mother had shared to collect the books. I found the door open, and Takeo Harada at the window. With its stripped beds, the room looked like a cell.

"Excuse me, I just came for the books."

He gestured to the neat stack of books on the chair. The Whitman and the Dickinson were there as well. Had he even read them? I wished I could suggest he keep these. He might find some consolation there. But there was such despair in his eyes, I didn't dare.

"Hazel," said Ada as I passed the reception desk. "He's looking for you."

Lytton Phelps waited for me on the steps of the Cottage. "Hazel, come in please." His voice sounded somber.

Had Joe finally told him, about me leaving the door open to the swimming pool? It was almost a relief—the secret was out. A child had died because I was careless. I deserved to be fired, punished.

"Come inside, please," he said. His tone was too gentle. He placed an arm across my shoulders and led me to the office.

I knew.

"Please, sit down," he said. "This came for you."

He held out a heavy cream-colored envelope. From the War Department.

Overseas authorities have done their utmost to secure information regarding missing personnel. Captured enemy reports have been examined and verified, in addition to lists of liberated prisoners of war. I regret to inform you that your husband has not been included in any report or list. Your husband's case has been reviewed in accordance with the provisions of Public Law 90, 77th Congress, as amended. This review has resulted in an official finding of death. Your loss is irreparable, and your grief is great. We trust the knowledge of your husband's devotion to duty may sustain and comfort you.

Although I had expected this for so long, the words on the page hit me like a blow.

Husband your resources, the Quakers say. My husband was gone. Such waste.

Lytton Phelps helped me to the door; I leaned on him like a child.

"I'll take you down to the hotel," he said.

"I'm all right, sir. I'll go on from here."

"Are you sure?"

"I'd rather." I concentrated on walking. One stiff step after the other. I made it to the garage.

Joe looked up from waxing the Packard. My tongue felt stiff and thick in my mouth—I couldn't frame the words, just handed him the letter.

He struck the hood of the car with his fist, so hard he left a dent in the shining surface. Then he rubbed his knuckles and waved his hand, shaking off the pain.

"I'll take you into town, to see his dad. Grace."

"Not yet," I said.

Joe steadied me all the way down the hill. I leaned on him,

smelling oil and wax, sweat.

On the kitchen steps, the girls were taking a smoke break. My face must have given me away. Cora wrapped her arms around me, murmured something into my hair.

I swayed, dizzy.

"Take her to lie down in my room," said Mrs. Johnson.

"No," I said. "I'd rather go up."

Cora and Joe together guided me up to my room.

"Do you want me to stay?" asked Cora.

"No. But thank you, both of you."

Neal's picture greeted me from the bureau—young and strong.

How did that Japanese poem go? *All the soldiers leave behind is grass.*

I sprayed myself with a mist of the *Apple Blossom* perfume he'd given me. I had been saving it for when he came back. I crawled into bed, and read his sparse letters and V-Mails.

> *I just got a batch of letters from you … Now I can just about account for every day since we said good-bye. I really appreciate your writing every day. I can't give you much info about the transport, but you'll get a kick out of the goody bags we received halfway across the ocean, courtesy of the Red Cross. Swell stuff—playing cards, stationery, cigarettes, shoelaces and a sewing kit! So when I come home, I'll do my own mending. I always have for Dad and me, anyway.*

> *Let's call our first little girl Hazel, unless you'd rather name her after your mother. But when I get back, we both need to go on to school, agreed? I used to think I wanted to get*

away from Bedford. I have to say, from here, it looks pretty
good to me now. But, we'll see, right? Anywhere I settle
down with you looks pretty good.

Images of the lost future unrolled like a spool of film spoilt by light. I buried the correspondence deep in the back of my lingerie drawer, with Gwendolyn Harada's pearls. I lay in bed, creasing and folding one of my father's handkerchiefs, unable to cry.

Later, Joe drove me into town. The car hummed along 220, arriving too soon. We passed the well-kept brick houses along Richard Street and Juliana Street, the Common School, the Courthouse. All stood solid and eternal. It struck me as so strange, the way places and things outlast people. Every block, every corner hurt me: the jeweler's, the movie theater. We crossed the river where he'd fished, and over the tracks, to the shabby clapboard house where Neal's father lived above the failed hardware store, beside the lumber yard. I would have postponed arriving at my father-in-law's door forever, done anything to escape my duty to ring his door bell.

I rang the bell.

Rang, and rang again.

"Guess he's out," said Joe. "Or out cold."

"One more time, and then we can go," I said.

But before I even touched the bell, he appeared, barely visible through the clouded, dirty oval glass of the door.

"Come in," he said. "I know why you're here."

Steep stairs led to his apartment above the store. The shades were down. He stank and his rooms stank, too—the ripe, rotting scent of alcoholic neglect. His dark green work pants sagged, a cord around his waist instead of a belt.

He wove and stumbled down the dark hallway to the parlor. Joe and I sat on a sofa bulging with broken springs.

"Have a drink," he said, "in my boy's honor."

He poured drinks. I could not bring myself to touch the scummy glass, but Joe drank.

"Neal was a great guy, sir," he said.

My father-in-law looked at him, his face slack, and poured himself another shot.

Every flat surface in the room was furred with dust. The grate was clogged with ash. No one had cleaned since Neal left.

"Drive past the Jail," I told Joe after we had escaped.

He pulled up across the street, across from the solid brick building. A shadow flickered behind a curtain, almost as though my father waited, looking out for me, holding supper for me on the back of the stove.

We stopped at Grace McKee's last.

"What a nice surprise," she began, but faltered as I stepped into the light of the hallway.

"Oh, my god," she said. I leaned on her shoulder, her clean lavender scent washed over me. But I still didn't cry.

Grace made us tea. We sat at the kitchen table where I sometimes used to do homework, waiting for my father to join us after my lesson for one of her suppers.

"You're not going back there," she said. "You're staying here."

The prospect tempted me, the thought of lying tucked into her clean, heavy sheets, like an ailing child, an invalid on bed rest. I would eat in bed on a tray or at the white porcelain topped kitchen table. I could hide here. The Japanese would go. I would forget the Harada family. I would forget Mia. I might even tell her about Mia. *Oh, how sad. But accidents happen,* I imagined her saying, kind and matter of fact.

"Soon," I said to Grace. "I'll come back, once they're gone. But there is a lot to do, Mr. Phelps needs me." In fact, it was the other way around. I needed to be busy, to have the illusion of purpose, a place in the world. I needed to wave good-bye until everyone, everyone, had disappeared.

"Take care of her, Joe," she said as we left.

"I've been trying," he said, with a wry smile.

"Do you have the gas to drive past the Ship?"

"Sure," he said.

The bar was still open; we didn't go in. I was here for the view: the height above the world, the distance from everything.

Why did you disappear into the sky? It was as though that Japanese poet from so long ago was speaking to me. She understood.

I heard music from the radio inside the bar, *Moonlight Serenade.*

"Neal and Glenn Miller went missing about the same time," I said to Joe.

He nodded, dropping a coin in the telescope. "Take a look through here," he said.

I looked down on the sparse twinkling lights of the valley below. Maybe the world looks like this when you leave it. As I stepped away from the telescope, for just the briefest of moments, I realized how easy it would be to fall—or jump—over the railing. The edge seemed to pull me. I shivered.

Joe put his jacket around my shoulders. "Time to go," he said.

The lights were blazing in the hotel as we turned in the drive. Joe paused at the sentry box.

"Why's it all lit up?" Joe asked the guard.

"Just got word—they're leaving tomorrow. Train to Chicago, then Seattle, then the boat."

"Tomorrow?" My heart was racing.

"Yes, ma'am." He stepped out of the booth and leaned in Joe's window, looking at me. It was the guard who usually sat at the desk when I went swimming. His face was serious, no trace of his grinning flirtation. "Sorry about your husband. The ultimate sacrifice."

For the first time it struck me—I was a widow after barely having time to be a bride, and no time to be a wife.

Joe drove toward the hotel.

"How does everyone know about Neal already?"

"Grapevine, Hazel. He'll be in the Honor Roll in the *Gazette* tomorrow."

"The ultimate waste," I said.

"I don't think Neal would want you to see it that way."

"Well, I do."

Joe stopped the car at the kitchen steps.

"No, I'll ride up the hill. I'm going up to the office," I said. "I'm sure he's busy."

My boss looked up from his desk, surprise and relief mingling on his face.

"Hazel, this is no time for you to be working."

"I'd rather."

Footsteps sounded on the porch and then the hallway. I heard a soft rapping on the office door. Nejiko Suwa entered, bowing nervously.

"Sir?" she said. "You sent for me? Is it—is it because I must leave my violin?"

"No," he said. "Keep it. But—promise me, if they trace the owner, you will return it."

"Thank you," she said, bowing. "I would like to play for you. One last time."

"I would like you to play for everyone. Tonight."

"It would be my honor. I will include the Mendelssohn." She bowed again.

Just before the last curfew of that last night, everyone assembled—prisoners and staff. We all stood together on the lawn, looking up at the lighted porch that served as Nejiko Suwa's stage. She played, and the strains of music, sad and lovely, floated down around us. The violin wept. The music drifted up the mountainside, up to the pavilion where Neal and I had kissed the first time. I imagined it wafting up and over the dark mountain, and disappearing. When she finally put down her bow for the last time I discovered my cheeks were wet with tears.

After the music ended, I watched as the crowd dispersed. Takeo Harada passed by the tree where I stood in the shadows. He did not notice me. His eyes looked straight ahead, the eyes that could never be wet with tears. I almost spoke then. I wanted to say I was so sorry that his family was gone. I wanted to say I knew what it was like to lose everyone you loved.

I wandered into the kitchen and found Mrs. Johnson arranging silver and polish on the long worktable.

"I'm at sixes and sevens," she said. "Polishing silver always settles my nerves."

"May I help you?" I asked.

She nodded. "Of course," she said.

We sat side by side, polishing silver. Spoons, knives, forks, spread out on the long battered wood table that ran the length of the big kitchen.

She was right; the repetitive motion, dipping the worn rag into the pot of paste, rubbing the tarnish away, eased my mind. I rubbed gritty pink paste into the bowls of the spoons, along the tines of the forks, the blades of the knives. The pink turned gray as the tarnish bled away.

I was sorry when we finished. After the last teaspoon was put away, she said, "Would you like a little nip of something? A hot toddy? It might help you sleep."

The tenderness in her eyes touched me. "No, thank you," I said. "But you were right. Polishing silver helps."

She nodded, satisfied. "I always wonder what people like Mrs. Roosevelt do. It must be terrible, not having any work to do, when bad things happen."

I climbed upstairs, stopping at each landing, walking down each balcony. This was the last night the detainees would sleep behind these doors. Their worn shoes waited outside the bedroom doors; this time tomorrow, the floor would be bare. The detainees would be gone. The hotel would be empty of guests once more.

On the third floor landing, Takeo Harada leaned against the balustrade opposite his door. If he heard my steps, he gave no sign as he gazed out toward the dark mountainside.

I should have continued up the stairs. I should have skirted around him. I should have been angry at him. Neal had died. He might have been tortured in a Japanese camp, for all I knew. But I didn't pass by.

Takeo Harada's sadness attracted mine, like a magnet.

"I learned my husband died today," I said.

"My condolences," he said. His tone was gentle—the way he spoke to Charlotte. He offered me a silver flask. For a moment as I took it, our fingers brushed together.

I sipped. Straight from the flask his lips had touched, leaving formality behind, as though we were simply sharing a tin cup at a well. The whiskey burned and I coughed, handing his flask back to him.

He bowed, crossed the balcony, and vanished into his room.

I leaned on the balustrade, listening to the mournful hooting of an owl and the stream murmuring below. The faint shadows of bats flitted under the eaves. I saw a shooting star. It was a warm night, but I was shivering, cold to the core in a way the whiskey couldn't touch.

I pushed his door open, and slipped into the room.

He sat on the side of his bed, holding something in his hands. "Go," he said. "Please."

"No." I crossed the room.

Takeo Harada stood and I saw he was holding a bowl, a dark pottery bowl covered with a sparkling, random pattern of gold.

I reached out to touch it. The golden pattern was raised, ridged, like the veins on a leaf.

"This bowl has been broken and mended many times. It has lasted. And so will you. Grief confuses you now. You must go," he said.

He turned away, and walked to a corner of the room and placed the bowl on the floor against the wall. He knelt, his back to me, and bowed his head.

I unbuttoned my blouse, tugging open the white mother-of-pearl buttons shaped like flowers. I took off my skirt, my slip, my underwear. I pulled back the government-issue blanket, the rough sheet, and crawled into the bed. Even under the heavy blanket, I shivered. Closing my eyes, I lay there, listening to his soft breathing across the room. It comforted me. I wept and drifted.

And then he was standing above the bed. "You must go," he said.

"Please, we're both alone, and I'm so cold." I opened the covers, reached up, and drew him down beside me.

He was smooth and cool as marble. He did not kiss me. He never kissed me. But he held me. We warmed each other. Much later, we made love, or went through the gestures of love, the act of love. It felt dark and strange, a necessary ritual of mourning and comfort.

Afterward, the blood pounded in my ears, coursed through my veins. *I'm alive!* I shouted silently. *I'm still alive.*

I fell asleep beside him and slept deeply, as though floating in a still pool. When I awoke it was to the gray light of early morning. I was alone. Once again, he knelt in the corner of the room, his back to me, his head bowed.

I dressed in furious haste. What had I done? It wasn't the one sip of whiskey. I had been drunk with grief—and what I had done had been crazy. I must be hidden safe in my room before anyone stirred.

I stepped barefoot onto the balcony.

Joe stood only feet away, at the foot of the stairs leading up to my room. He held a bunch of goldenrod and Queen Anne's lace. His eyes narrowed and his lips pressed into a hard line.

"These were for you," he said, tossing the flowers over the balustrade. Leaning on the railing, he limped down the stairs.

I ran upstairs. Neal's photograph stared at me from the bureau.

"Forgive me," I said, and turned the picture to the wall.

I bathed in a scalding hot tub, scrubbing fiercely. Would Joe denounce me? I imagined public humiliation, had a vision of being paraded with Takeo Harada around the grounds of the hotel for everyone to see. I remembered that other woman, the one in Emmitsburg who'd run off with her German POW. The papers called her a traitor, a collaborator. The girls at the hotel whispered another word—whore.

After my bath, I dressed carefully. I tried to pull my rings off, the rings I didn't deserve. But my fingers were swollen. Though I slicked my hands with lather, I could not slip the rings over my knuckle.

In the mirror, I looked no different from the morning before, no visible sign that in the past twenty-four hours I had learned I was a widow, and betrayed my husband. I packed my suitcase, ready to be expelled.

"Sure you don't want to take the day off?" asked Prudence Johnson, kindly, when I entered the kitchen.

I shook my head.

Cora said, "I've fixed his breakfast—would you like me to take it to him?"

"No," I said. "I'll do it."

My boss was deep in a telephone discussion. I sat at my typewriter, staring blankly out the window. He hung up the phone. He was coming to my desk.

I looked down at my hands, twisting my rings. "I didn't expect you this morning," Mr. Phelps said kindly. "You may certainly be excused."

So Joe had said nothing. Kept my secret. Protected me, again.

"Please—I'd rather be busy," I said.

The buses for the detainees would come by mid-morning. When I carried the paperwork down to the front desk, I found the hotel humming with the energy of departure. Children ran up and down the stairs, excited. The Japanese queued for their funds from the commissary, carried down their bags.

The blue and gold buses arrived. I stood on the porch. Cora had linked her arm through mine, consoling. Ada protected my other flank. I didn't deserve the support they were giving me. But I needed it. Joe was down on the lawn, pushing a wheelbarrow loaded with suitcases to the drive. *Thank you,* I thought. *Thank you.*

The detainees formed a long line across the lawn waiting to be called to have their papers stamped, passports returned. I experienced a sense of déjà vu, as though seeing a newsreel of their arrival played backward.

"How long is it going to take them to get there?" asked Cora.

"Weeks," said Ada. "First Cumberland, then Chicago, then change trains for Seattle. Then the boat—weeks and weeks."

"Isn't it funny, to think you have to go West to go East?" said Cora.

The Ambassador and his wife boarded the first bus. She wore a long black coat. He carried a furled umbrella dangling from his wrist.

"Look at him," said Ada. "He looks—he looks like he *won*. Say what you like, Japs are strange."

The roll call began.

Anesaki, Arai, Atusane, Bamba, Dazai, Doi.

Harada ... Harada!

Takeo Harada did not step forward.

Harada, Harada.

"Where's Harada? Go get him, Joe!" Lytton Phelps barked through a megaphone.

Oh no, I thought. Joe would be alone with Takeo Harada, in his room. What would Joe say? What would happen now? I shivered.

"Oh, honey," said Cora. "Are you sure you don't want to go lie down?"

"No!" I said, shaking free of her comforting touch.

The roll call continued.

Mitsuno. Mia's mother, supported by one woman, had to be coaxed onto the bus by another woman. Her daughter's ashes would be sent on from the crematorium in Pittsburgh.

Suwa. The young woman stepped toward the bus, violin clasped to her breast. Good-bye, princess of the cherry blossoms. I hope you find—I hope you find that your friend has survived.

"There's Joe," said Cora. "But where's Mr. Harada?"

Joe spoke to Mr. Phelps. My boss went onto the bus himself then, and came out with the Ambassador.

"What's going on?" said Ada.

Phelps and Oshima hurried inside the hotel.

"Something's wrong," said Cora.

The guards continued the roll-call. Everyone was on board. Still, no sign of the Ambassador, or Mr. Phelps. Or of Takeo Harada.

"You know," said Ada, "I bet that Mr. Harada is insisting on going to England. I bet he's like on strike, you know? I mean—wasn't it peculiar, the way he just let them go without a fuss?"

"The Japanese believe you shouldn't make a fuss," I said.

"Well, believe you me, if someone tried to separate me from my kid and my spouse, I'd fuss!" said Ada.

The Ambassador crossed the lawn alone and boarded the bus again. The motors roared and the convoy pulled down the driveway.

They were leaving Takeo Harada behind! Had—had Joe told Mr. Phelps about what we had done? Was he being held behind as punishment? I swayed, a little dizzy.

"Hazel, honey, you really should sit down," said Cora.

But just then, Mr. Phelps came up to me.

"Hazel, I need you to come with me," he said. His tone was very grave.

We walked up the hill. I was afraid to speak, afraid to ask any questions.

"We have something very unfortunate on our hands, I'm afraid," he said.

I swallowed, preparing myself.

"I need your help, with letters and arrangements. Takeo Harada has died."

"Died?" I stumbled.

"Suicide. Hung himself with a bed sheet."

The sheet we lay on, betraying my husband and his wife. It was my fault. Greedy for comfort, I had shamed him. And Joe had discovered him, hanging from that shameful sheet. But he must have kept my secret. He hadn't told Lytton Phelps about seeing me leaving that room. Loyalty takes many forms. His silence was as much a gift to Neal as to me.

I sighed, a deep, shuddering sigh.

"I know," my boss said. "It's terrible, most unfortunate. Somehow, I feel at fault. Should have anticipated this sort of thing. They have such a stringent sense of honor. Defeat is unthinkable."

My knees almost gave way, I stumbled again.

"Careful," said Mr. Phelps. "Don't twist your ankle."

Later, my boss met with the Sheriff.

"I was afraid of this, given what we were dealing with. Their whole code of honor, you know. Look at the kamikazes," Mr. Phelps said. "But—I knew they had no weapons. I should have taken steps."

"If someone is crazy enough to be bent on doing himself in, nothing you can do to stop it. You read the cover story in *Life*? About how the Jap mind takes defeat?" the Sheriff asked.

"Fate worse than death to them," said Mr. Phelps. "It could have been worse. At least it was only one of them. Could have had an epidemic of ritual suicide after the surrender."

One is too many, I wanted to shout. Takeo Harada didn't kill himself over Japan being defeated! He lost his wife and child. I made him betray his wife. I was to blame. The shame he couldn't bear was my fault.

"How about the note Joe found?" asked the Sheriff.

I stiffened. A note?

"He wanted his ashes sent to Nagasaki. Talk about ashes to ashes. And to send his personal effects to the widow in England."

"Well, at least she and the kid were spared being here for this," said the Sheriff.

"There's that," said Phelps. "Between you and me, I'm not looking forward to the inquest. Filing my report on this. Maybe it couldn't have been prevented, but it happened on my watch. I'm responsible." He sounded worried. Might this be bad for his career? He'd tried to be fair to them. Look at all the trouble I'd caused.

While my boss walked the Sheriff back to the hotel, I typed up the notes from their meeting. Afterward, I tidied my desk, covered my Underwood, procrastinating heading to the hotel myself until there was nothing left to do.

As I passed the garage, Joe stepped out, blocking my path.

I should thank him. Apologize. Ask him to forgive me. My throat locked shut.

"He left something for you. I put it in the glove of the Olds." He stood there, looking at me, looking through me with his pale grey eyes, until I flinched and looked away.

He thrust out his fist. I recoiled as though he would strike me. Joe gave a snort and opened his hand. He dropped a button, a flower-shaped button from my blouse, into the dust.

"Believe this is yours," he said. He ground the button under his heel and limped down the hill.

The garage was dark, and smelled of dirt and gasoline. The car gleamed in the half-light. I opened the glove box gingerly, as though an animal might be trapped inside and bite me.

Takeo Harada's black bowl rested on the pile of folded maps. The gold seams gleamed inside the dark glove box.

Inside the bowl I found a small scrap of translucent rice paper, folded on an angle:

For Hazel Shaw: What is broken is also beautiful.

Epilogue
April, 1985

The hotel gong clangs. A fire! A drowning! I've left a door open!

I struggle awake and swim back to the surface of the present moment out of the deep dream of the past. The school breakfast bell is ringing. I'm at Clear Spring. It's Saturday morning, time to go pick up Charlotte for our trip to the Springs. There is no emergency—except the bottomless situation with Jacques.

Morning light floods through the lace curtains and prints a shadow tattoo on the glossy wood floor. Barefoot, I walk to the window and look out down the hillside to the pond. The gate I insisted on is securely shut beside the sign—*No Swimming Unattended.* The thickening leaves in the trees at the far edge of the pond almost hide the faculty houses from view. Over there, Jacques and Angelique are waking up—if they've slept. There must be a way to protect them, without putting Clear Spring in jeopardy. Should I call Charlotte and cancel? Tell her I cannot go with her to the Springs? Leave her to face the past alone?

I wish I could call Ted. *You need to get some perspective,* I imagine him saying. *You know what happens with the forest and the trees. Go.*

Breakfasting barefoot on the patio, I watch the scarlet tanager dart back and forth to its nest in the shrubbery, a touch of brilliance on the campus, like Jacques and Angelique. The *Post* says the blossoms at the Tidal Basin will peak on Monday, just in time for the coronation of the Cherry Blossom Princess at the festival. I remember Nejiko Suwa, playing her violin that last evening. The gentle intensity with which she touched the strings; the almost unbearably sad melody she drew out of it.

There isn't much to pack, for a one night stand with the past: night clothes, bathing suit, a cashmere sweater. The spring evening will be chilly, there in the foothills of the Alleghenies. Opening my jewelry box, I choose my mother's locket. Somehow the rose gold is always warm to the touch. My fire opal engagement ring glints—I never wear it. But now I force it on the ring finger of my right hand, pushing it over a knuckle thickened with age. I open a silk pouch and run the lustrous strand of Gwendolyn Harada's milky pearls through my fingers. The jeweler who restrung them a few years back suggested insuring the necklace, surprising me with his estimate of its value. I wear them on special occasions, when I need courage, dignity. The necklace puts a little extra starch in my backbone. I tuck the pearls in my cosmetics bag.

Travelling light into the past, but there is one more essential item. I hold the bowl, tracing the gold seams that tell its story of damage and restoration. I wrap it in layers of tissue, and nestle it in my case.

The maintenance man is already repainting the school sign at the end of the driveway, mending the vandalism. Soon it will say *Clear Spring Friends School* again, not *Clear Spring   ends School.* I smile, wave and speed away, chasing the shadows of the telephone wires along the road. The top is down and the merciful wind whips my thoughts into the air.

Charlotte's sabbatical rental in Foggy Bottom stands on an anonymous block of the dull neighborhood, convenient to the

Kennedy Center and the insidious sprawl of George Washington University. She's waiting outside in a scarlet raincoat with a draping collar, bright as a geisha against the drab building.

"Should I put my case in the boot?"

I keep the interior of my car, like the public areas of my house, impeccable. But the trunk holds a jumble of books, papers, and discarded clothes intended for the Meeting's thrift shop.

"Excuse the mess in the trunk," I say.

"What a fabulous car," she says, fastening her seat belt, smiling at me.

"It's a little ridiculous, but I love it," I reply.

"I have a Mini. It's my pet." Again, a quick smile, almost mischievous. She so rarely smiled, then.

We swoop past the Lincoln Memorial, between the gilded horses guarding Memorial Bridge, and cross the Potomac.

"Look back—see the cherry blossoms," I tell her.

"What a lovely city. It reminds me of Paris."

"Thanks to L'Enfant. Have you been here before?"

She's tying her scarf as I remember. She has been here, at least once before. But not as a tourist.

"Only that once," she says. "With my mother, on our way to England."

I watch the road. The George Washington Parkway runs along a high escarpment above the Potomac, protected from the cliff by a low stone wall. On the radio the notes of a Mozart horn concerto are ripped away by the breeze.

"Do you mind?" she asks, leaning forward to turn up the volume.

Washington disappears behind us across the river. We cruise west. The suburbs give way to fields, farmhouses, stone barns, and cows. We lose the radio signal.

"Antietam Battlefield." she says, reading the sign.

"These were all Civil War battlefields along here. They say the streams ran red with blood. I bring my Peace Studies kids here."

"What's the curriculum for your course?"

"Primary sources, as much as possible. Letters. Diaries. Speakers."

"Who comes to talk about World War II?"

My eyes are tearing; it must be from the wind. I put on my sunglasses. "Several people. One is a member of the Meeting. He was a conscientious objector, a medic in Germany, right up to the end." I stop. This is so close to what's between us.

"Go on," she says.

"He treated soldiers not much older than my kids. One of the boys, dying after the Bulge, told him he was afraid he'd go to hell, for killing. The boy said if he had it to do over again, he'd be a C.O." A semi-truck hurtles past us, honking. I am shaking. I put my flashers on and pull over to the side of the road. "My C.O. was with the troops liberating Buchenwald. He tells my kids—remember, he's a Quaker—that after seeing the camp and the survivors, he lost his belief in pacifism. That what he saw was so evil he wished he'd fought against it."

Charlotte is looking at me intently, her gray eyes glinting green in the bright sun.

"It must be powerful, for your students, to learn things are not so cut and dried. Who else comes?"

"A lawyer. Jewish, grew up in Berlin. The Quakers sponsored him, got him out in 1938. He served in our Air Force. Took depositions from the camp guards, before Nuremberg. He says the big guns were after the big fish."

"Like Ambassador Oshima," she says.

"Yes. But he says people like himself, lower down the chain, found ways not to let the petty villains get off. To take justice into their own hands."

"How?"

"Took them to displaced persons camps. Left them there. For—

debriefing by the survivors. No one ever saw them again."

"My father might have been at Nuremberg," she says, "The shame would have killed my mother." She sighs, shakes her head. "And do you—do you talk about the Japanese internment camps at all?"

"A Nisei woman comes. She was a senior in high school—applied to college while living in a horse stall with her family."

"All my father's Japanese friends in England were interned on the Isle of Wight," she says.

"I remember your mother telling me that."

"Really?" She looks at me. "Do you tell your kids—I like how you call them that—about us?"

"I haven't," I say. "I should try." It's such a complicated story, I want to say. The truth is I've not been brave enough.

"Maybe I could come, we could tell them together." She hands me a tissue. I blot my eyes.

"I never cry," I say. "I know someone who had to see a lachrimologist—her eyes were so dry. I could be that person."

"Neither do I. My father said—the eyes of a daughter of the samurai must never be wet."

"I remember."

A bus roars past us. Is she also remembering the blue and gold buses from Cumberland, with the blacked out windows? I ease off the shoulder and return to the highway. We drive beneath the footbridge for the Appalachian Trail, climbing into the mountains of western Maryland. A hawk soars overhead.

We pass the billboard at the border: "*Pennsylvania Welcomes You!*"

"Fancy being welcome here," Charlotte says. "My mother would never believe it."

"How is she?"

"Gone a year. Cancer."

"I'm sorry." I glance across. She has her sunglasses on again, a shield.

"I wouldn't have prolonged her suffering," said Charlotte. "She thought she'd lived much more than long enough. My mother never found much happiness, afterwards." Her tone is even.

"I'm sorry," I say, like a broken record.

The Breezewood interchange sprawls at the confluence of Interstate 70, the Turnpike, and Route 30. A glut of motels, gas stations, and fast food restaurants blights the landscape like alluvial detritus left by the flood of travelers and truckers.

"Ugly," I apologize to Charlotte. "We get off onto the old road, Route 30."

We pass a billboard for Iron City Beer and an abandoned brick tavern at the crest of the hill. Then the road sweeps down and runs along the Juniata River. *Bait,* reads a hand lettered sign beside an old-fashioned motor court. Along the river bank, camping trailers and fishing shacks cluster. For a moment I can feel and smell the cool, dark cabin where I spent my brief honeymoon. A junk shop by the side of the road has an incongruous plaster elephant, almost life size, among the rusty gliders and lawn chairs. A barn emblazoned with *Chew Mail Pouch Tobacco* sits in a rocky field. We drive past the hospital—it's larger than I recall. Next, a new shopping plaza with gas stations and big box stores.

Crossing the river over the bridge at The Narrows, I see a car parked with a canoe on the roof-rack. I glance down at the water and imagine Neal in his waders. An unfamiliar sign offers a choice: *Business Route 30* or *Bedford Bypass.*

We drive into town, past the fairgrounds. The Coffee Pot looks vacant. Tarpaper shingles peel off its curved walls. "I worked there, before the Springs," I tell her. Further down the block in town, Dunkle's Gas is still the gleaming art deco temple I recall.

"I went to school with one of the Dunkles," I say.

In the Square, the Civil War soldier still stands watch on his granite pedestal, looking down on Lawyer's Row, the Presbyterian Church, the Lutheran Church, the post office. If I stay on Juliana Street now we'll come to the Common School, and then be on our way to the Springs. Or if I turn here, we'll pass the Jail.

"It hasn't changed much at all," I say. "Preserved by lack of money and industry. And it helps to be a county seat. The courthouse dome over there is modeled on one by Sir Christopher Wren."

We pass the Courthouse where I married Neal on that hot summer afternoon a lifetime ago. No, that's wrong—in another lifetime. I was another person then. No one else, no one else has ever looked at me the way he did that day. The way I remember her father looked at her mother, as Gwendolyn played.

I drive through the Square and straight past the Common School, past Grace McKee's and out of town. I drive fast or I will lose my nerve. If I turn around, I could be back at Clear Spring in three hours, safe from the unexploded landmines here.

The road hugs the river. I'd forgotten the soft, recumbent roll of the mountains and the way they form a narrow valley with natural protective walls—perfect for the State Department's purposes. We pass the Elks Club. It has a swimming pool now. We reach Naugel's Mill where Neal and I left our bikes before sneaking onto the Springs property.

The Bedford Springs appears like a mirage, stretching along the right side of the road: the gingerbread white balconies, the parade of pillars along the porch. Neither of us speaks. I drive beneath the metal footbridge that spans the road, turn into the driveway, and pull beneath the portico. Turning off the car, I sit for a moment in the quiet. I remember the rumble of the buses arriving that morning forty years before. I can see the arrogant Ambassador, the children on the lawn, a shy school girl with auburn hair, a red-haired woman whose shapely legs made Joe whistle, and a beautiful man.

"Ma'am? Excuse me? Checking in?" A young man leans in the window. He's blond and freckled, hair slicked back. A farm boy's strong neck bursts above the collar of his white shirt. He carries our suitcases. The steps sag a bit with the sponginess of incipient rot. They need painting, and so does the porch. In fact, at close range the hotel looks shabby. It's like discovering age spots and wrinkles on an old friend's face after a long absence.

Charlotte drops into one of the hickory and oak rocking chairs. "Just the same," she says.

Yes, at least the view itself is unchanged. We sit together, rocking, looking across the lawn, up at the dark, forested mountain. When we go inside, I see the gong is still there. I touch the cool engraved surface. The mallet hangs beside it. Do they use it?

"Tempted?" whispers Charlotte beside me.

A huge chandelier sparkles above our heads.

"I don't remember that," she says.

"It was wrapped up in muslin," I explain. "Lots of things were put away."

"So we wouldn't damage them," she says, a little bitter.

"Well, there was the Mountain Navy here, before."

We approach the desk where Ada ruled the switchboard. A huge bowl of peonies and roses almost hides the receptionist. I blink to clear my vision, seeing double; the present room hangs like a scrim between me and the ghost room of the past.

"Good morning," the receptionist says. "Welcome to the Springs." I take in her clear skin and open countenance. She's too plump and genuinely pleasant for a front desk job in Washington.

Charlotte takes charge with quiet authority. She has perfect posture in her scarlet coat, from the crown of her head down her back, down the tapered legs. A diplomat's daughter. A performer's daughter.

"Charlotte Bledsoe. I've booked two rooms."

"But we'll be paying separately." I slide my credit card on the smooth wooden counter, looking across at the pigeon holes for mail and keys. Empty, but still there.

"I love your accent," the girl says to Charlotte. "Like Princess Di."

She signs the guest book with her full name, Charlotte Harada Bledsoe. Signing, I wonder if anyone will recognize her father's name—or mine. Unlikely. Prudence Johnson would be at least one hundred. It was indeed another lifetime.

The sturdy bellhop leads us to the elevators.

"I don't recall a lift," Charlotte says.

"It's always been here. Maybe you visited us when it was out of order. That happens," he says, with a chuckle.

The bellhop wasn't born when we were last here. And we weren't visitors. But I don't enlighten him. I won't remind Charlotte that she doesn't recall the elevator because these corridors were off limits. We only used the exterior stairs, so the guards could keep track.

The elevator shudders to a stop.

"This way, ladies."

Our rooms are on the third floor in the oldest wing of the rambling hotel. He unlocks the door to my room and pulls up the shades to reveal the balcony.

I had never expected to look out these windows again.

"You're right next door, ma'am," he says to Charlotte. I tip him.

My spacious room is furnished simply. The double bed sports a white counterpane. There is a wing chair and a drop leaf table. No television—not good, for attracting guests. I turn on the clock radio and discover static. Reception was better for us, thanks to the Mountain Navy. The closet door turns out to be the entrance to a small bathroom. A necessary upgrade. What modern guest would walk down the balcony to a shared bath? The renovation might have been just post-war, judging by the small porcelain sink and tub—

adequate, but nothing luxurious. Perhaps it was the work of the new manager afterward. I taste the bitter bubbles of the champagne Mrs. Johnson brought with his compliments the long night of VJ Day.

I find Charlotte on the balcony, leaning against the balustrade, gazing at Evitt's Mountain across the road. There's the familiar sound of rushing water below in Shober's Run. We could be standing on the spot where I encountered her father that last night. A hawk circles over the evergreen ridge.

"I wonder if he's the hawk we saw on the drive up," she says.

"Raptors love the air currents here."

Our rooms are at the far end of the building. Rocking chairs line the balcony. Beyond the hotel, the green expanse of the golf course stretches to the Alleghenies. Only a few golfers populate the landscape. This is not exactly a thriving resort.

"Feels like we're the only guests. May be good you got me back here when you did," I say.

We have lunch in the bar. The main dining room is only open for dinner, another sign of hard times.

Two middle-aged men, golfers, sit on stools at the bar. This end of the porch has been enclosed and a group of golf widows are laughing over drinks. We sit at a small round table by the windows, near the pool table and an upright piano.

Charlotte stares out the window, her sculpted features remind me of her father. I've seen no trace of her mother's drama. On the lawn there's a horseshoe pit, badminton net, and a swing dangles from the broad branch of a huge maple. Does she also see her father and the other men, pacing their circular laps behind the haughty Ambassador?

Our waitress is another healthy, pretty girl. Her white uniform is snug.

"It seems quiet here," I say.

"We get busy after Memorial Day. This is a great place for

weddings. This year the Pittsburgh Symphony is going to play in the field by the mill."

Encouraging news, delivered with the optimism of youth. She's probably fresh out of high school, but won't go to college, though Western Maryland College is not that far from here. Some of my kids go there. If the Jacques thing blows up, what will happen to our hard-won progress with college placement? My thoughts slip back to school.

"Ma'am? What will you have?"

Charlotte has already ordered. I ask for a club sandwich. We share a pot of tea which comes in one of the pots Prudence Johnson had kept locked up with all the hotel dishes. The sandwiches are served on the hotel china, too, decorated with the Duke of Bedford's crest and his odd motto: *Che sera sera.*

"The Japanese say, 'out with the water'," Charlotte says, tracing the words.

"Like we say, 'no good crying over spilt milk.'"

"No, it's more like acquiescence—let it go. Let it flow. Let it wash away."

I ponder. "But even letting go requires action, in a way. Relinquishing. Not crying over spilt milk is more passive, fatalistic. Just the opposite of the Western/Eastern stereotypes."

She smiles, that subtle, wry smile. "Stereotypes—can be misleading."

We go for a walk after lunch, carrying gnarled walking sticks from the umbrella stand—replicas from the glory days of the hotel. The footbridge that once reached from the second floor balcony across the road to the trailhead has been partially dismantled. All that remains is a short section of walkway accessible from the lawn. We climb the stairs and cross above the road and over the stream, Shober's Run.

"We never used this footbridge," she says.

"It was locked," I say.

"Off limits? Like—the pool?"

"Yes."

We sit in the white frame gazebo on the mountainside, where she and I sat that one afternoon, where Neal and I used to sit. The hotel complex stretches below us. It's a stage set for ghosts from another time. From this distance, the white gingerbread woodwork on the balconies glistens and the lawn looks lush. The circular scar worn into the grass by the Japanese men walking their laps has healed and disappeared.

We begin to climb and reach the first spring. Rhododendrons cluster around the rough stone basin. The leaves are glossy with health, nourished by the mineral water.

Bridal Grotto says the sign.

I dip my fingers into the matted collage of brown leaves and pine needles on the surface of the water. The fire opal of my ring gleams.

"Your husband?" she says.

"He didn't come back."

If she had pressed me, I would not have said anything more, but she sat quiet, listening.

"The official letter came—declaring him dead. Right after you left."

"What happened?"

"I never knew. He went missing in the Battle of Leyte."

"Did you ever think—that they could be wrong?"

"No. I had known already, in a way. The letter made it real." I remember the heavy paper in my hands. I remember how cold I was. How I ached for him to hold me—for someone to hold me.

Charlotte is swishing her slender fingers through the water, back and forth, looking down into the basin. "My baby stopped moving, just before my due date. No heartbeat. The doctor said to wait and go into labor. Best chance for the baby, if it were still alive. I knew it was dead—but I couldn't quite give up. Afterward, they let me hold him. He'd be twenty now." She's weeping, my dry-eyed daughter of the samurai, leaning her head on my shoulder. I stroke her hair, inhaling the fragrance of sandalwood soap and something else. Incense?

"My marriage broke up. I went to Japan, on sabbatical. There are shrines in Kyoto, on the corners; stones wearing red bibs. For stillborn babies. I left one, for my baby, Takeo."

She'd named him for her father.

I am afraid to ask, but I must. "Did you find any of your family?"

"I went to Nagasaki, but no. I visited in August for Obon, the festival for the dead. I was there for the ceremony, and for the anniversary of the bomb."

"They still light the lanterns, on the bay? To guide the spirits home?"

"How do you know?"

"Your father told me."

She looked at me, a long considering look. "You talked about that?"

This is dangerous. "After Chef Takano died."

"Mr. Takano. Sweet man. His niece runs his family's *ryokan* in Kyoto."

"What happened to his wife and son?"

"His niece never heard from either of them. Maybe they stayed in France. She has no idea."

We follow the trail up the mountainside. Wildflowers push through the leaves on the forest floor. I name them for Charlotte as I did that other day: Trout Lily, Lady Slipper, Spring Beauties, Quaker Ladies. The warm air smells resinous. Growing in pine needles I find the ghostly pale translucent flutes. "These are Indian Pipes," I say.

"They call them Foreigners Pipes in Japan."

The lake has become a bog. Reeds swallow the shoreline. The

diving tower and float have been dismantled or rotted away. Gingerly we walk out on the weathered dock beside the deserted boathouse.

"Careful," I say.

"When you brought me here," she says. "It was—the only time I felt free."

Glittering dragonflies hover, latched together in mid-air.

"Mating," I say.

"Risky proposition," she says, with a small smile.

"Maybe that's part of the thrill."

We laugh. A great blue heron lifts off and takes graceful flight across the bog.

Retracing our path, we pause again in the pavilion, looking down through the screen of gray beech branches hazed with new leaves. Below, the afternoon sun catches the band of clerestory windows above the hotel swimming pool.

"Poor Mia," she says.

"There's a pond at my school. I fenced it in. All my kids have to pass a swim test."

"I brought a swimming suit with me."

"So did I."

"I'm a little afraid to swim there," she says.

"Me too."

"It seems like we should," she says. "Sort of—a ritual? A gesture?"

We change in our rooms and meet in the hallway, dressed like sisters in the hotel's thick white terry robes. The receptionist explains our room keys open the pool door. A sign posted beside the glass doors to the pool warns: *No Guard on Duty. No Children Unattended.* The bright rectangle of blue water glistens like hard candy. A few tiles around the edge of the floor are chipped but the basket weave pattern is still intact. The stairway to the upstairs balcony is roped off.

She looks into the pool, as though looking for someone at the bottom.

"I refused to swim for a while. The girls at my school called me a yellow Jap coward."

"Kids can be cruel."

"Especially to the nail that sticks out. I wanted to blend in. Still do, in a way. Like using my married name," she says, rueful.

Without her robe I see how very thin she is. We dangle our feet in the soft water—piped in from the springs, warmed by the hotel's furnace. Her feet are slender and almost translucent. Mine are sturdier peasant feet.

"I tried to find Mia's mother in Japan. No trace."

I recall the woman keening over her daughter's body, prone on these tiles.

"It was my fault," she says, "Mia followed me."

"No, I left the door open."

She shakes her head and sighs. "So we're both guilty. Or it was fate. This is a pilgrimage, isn't it? A way of trying to let the past go. To let it go. Out with the water."

She slips into the pool first and begins to swim, strong smooth strokes. I follow.

"You're a good swimmer," I say, afterward. Swaddled in our robes, we lounge on wicker chaises.

"My father taught me, before they closed the swimming baths in Berlin."

Shafts of light from the clerestory windows above gleam down on the water.

"Reminds me of the baths at the Takanos' *ryokan*," she says. "It's almost on the grounds of the Nasenji Temple. His niece reminded me of him—kind, but particular. The first day I wrapped my *yukata* the wrong way—the way you wrap a corpse, apparently. She set me straight!"

We laugh.

I close the door firmly behind us when we leave.

Dressing for dinner in my light wool slacks and my cashmere sweater, I suddenly miss Ted. He teases me it's against Quaker simplicity to love silk and cashmere so much. I look at the phone by my bed. But he's home by now, with his family.

I should call Abel, Jacques. But what more can I say? What, oh what, should I do?

Charlotte's tapping on my balcony door. I'm grateful for the interruption. She's elegant in a long gray tunic over narrow black trousers. I admire her without a trace of envy—as though she were my sister, or a daughter.

"Cocktail? Suntory," she says, holding up a silver flask.

His flask.

"Your father's!" I say, startled.

She studies me, pensive. "I found it while clearing out Mother's house. Apparently, the hotel sent us his things, but she hid them. Even my doll—my broken doll. I'd left it with him, to take to Japan for the ceremony Mr. Takano told me about."

"But she'd told you he was dead?"

"Eventually, and how he died. She blamed it on what she called his crazy allegiance to the Emperor. I believed—still believe—it was because we left him. She did, too, really, I think."

"No, what he did wasn't your fault."

"We abandoned him."

"He wanted you both to be safe. You were a child, you had no choice."

She sips from the flask. "At least now I have a few of his things."

"I'll be right back," I say. It's time.

Inside, I open my suitcase. I unwrap the bowl and hold it gently in my hands.

Charlotte is rocking, eyes on the mountain across the way.

"This is yours," I say, offering it to her.

"His bowl," she says.

"I—I found it after he was gone. I should have sent it on," I say. The weight of what remains unsaid pushes like water against a dam.

But she is not listening. She is staring at the bowl, rapt. "He kept this in his *tokonoma*, his shrine, in our parlor in Berlin." Charlotte traces the web of golden seams with her finger. "*Kintsugi*," she says. "Golden joinery. My favorite style in all of Japanese ceramics—because the damage isn't disguised."

"Experience—that's what's beautiful," I say, noticing the fine lines around her eyes, the crease at the corner of her mouth, the faint furrow across her smooth forehead. The sculptural balance of her features reminds me of him. The flaws of age enhance her loveliness.

"I've always wondered what the characters say. Did he know?" I ask her.

"I doubt it, such ancient kanji. He told me it had been re-broken many times on purpose so artists could repair the cracks. The more damage, the more gold seams, the more valuable."

She holds the bowl in the slanting evening light and its surface shimmers like brocade. I notice her wrists. The small, fine boned wrists bear faint scars—a delicate purple tracery. The vestigial calligraphy of an attempt, the vertical slashes that signal deadly intent. As I know, from a student we lost.

Charlotte catches me looking. She puts the bowl on the small table between our chairs and extends her hands, palms up, wrists exposed. "Yes, I tried my father's solution. After my baby died." She is struggling back tears. "The eyes of a daughter of the samurai," she says, with her gentle, rueful smile. Charlotte pours the Japanese whiskey into the cap of her father's flask and offers it to me.

The dining room glows with candlelight on tables covered with heavy white linen. There are tulips in cut glass. We are the only diners. How can this place keep going? Like my school, it must be struggling against a tide of red in the budget. I think of Jacques, Abel, of the developers waiting to swoop down on the fields at Clear Spring.

Our young waitress from lunch seats us at a table beside the long French windows: Ambassador Oshima's spot.

She recites the evening specials with enthusiasm. This girl enjoys her job, not like bored city girls waiting tables until something better comes along. "We have Bedford County turkey," she says. "And our salad greens are grown right here." She interrupts herself, as though remembering instructions not to rush the customers. "I can come back if you'd like a little more time."

"No, we're ready, I think," I say. "Do you have a wine list?"

"We have white or red," she says, proudly. "From California."

"Do you have champagne?" Charlotte asks.

I remember VJ night, and the bottle Prudence Johnson carried up the hill in a silver bucket.

"Yes," she says, blue eyes wide. "Is this a special occasion?"

"A reunion of old friends," Charlotte says.

The waitress takes our order, studiously noting our preferences for salad dressing. Tucking the pad in her apron pocket, she hurries toward the kitchen door. I can feel the swinging door with my own hip. I imagine Prudence Johnson in the kitchen, keeping an eye on everything and everyone with her constant critical attention.

Beyond the porch, across the road, mist is rising from the river. Dusk darkens into evening and the air thickens to twilight.

Our waitress returns, pops the cork, and pours for Charlotte to taste.

"Fine, thank you."

I raise my glass. "To absent friends," I say. Grace McKee's toast at my wedding supper.

Neither of us is, after all, very hungry, although the food is good and nicely presented on the hotel china. I cannot shake the sensation of being watched, as though Prudence Johnson, or someone, is nearby. Glancing at the porthole window in the swinging door, I do glimpse someone, with white hair, peering out. Whoever the apparition is, she disappears.

We decline dessert, to our waitress's dismay.

"Sometimes people come here just for the brownie sundae," she says. "There's coffee in the lounge," she offers, like a consolation prize.

There are oriental carpets on the floor, and comfortable leather chairs and sofas. A jigsaw puzzle in progress sits on a round table, so at least someone comes here. And there are books on the shelves of the lounge—local history.

"Do you know what happened, to those Japanese poetry books?" asks Charlotte.

"I'm not sure."

She approaches the grand piano. "The same one," she says.

"Do you play?"

"Not like she did. A little."

She begins. It's Chopin. I sink into the deep sofa and close my eyes. Charlotte is too modest. It could almost be Gwendolyn Harada on the piano bench. I miss Nejiko Suwa, the resonant tone of her Strad.

"Coffee?"

A woman with a crown of white braids in a tailored black dress stands beside the silver urn on the buffet. I hadn't heard her come into the room.

"Thank you," I say, starting to my feet.

"No need to get up," she says, "I'll bring it. Cream or sugar?" Her voice is familiar—it's more than the just the open vowels of the local accent.

"Just black." She bends down to hand me the cup of coffee, and I recognize the eyes, the kind smile.

"Cora!"

"Welcome back, Hazel. I'm the manager now. Saw your name on the register. Couldn't believe it."

Charlotte has spun around on the bench.

"And you must be the little Harada gal, all grown up."

A slender man with gray hair, leaning on a cane, appears in the doorway. His features have sharpened over the years. His face has the taut look of someone always in low-level pain.

"Joe," I say, goose-bumps rising on my arms.

He nods. "How do you do, Hazel." The tone is careful, so formal.

Again that sense of years dissolving as we exchange a long look. I am bone-cold.

Cora puts a proprietary hand on his arm. They're married, I realize.

"Joe's the chief engineer," she announces.

"Fancy dress title for maintenance," he says.

"It's hard keeping up with things. It's for sale again," she says with a worried frown. "We're hoping for the best."

"Mr. Gardner's gone?"

"It's his great-nephew's now. Absentee owner again. Doesn't work, for a place like this," she says. "I should get back to the kitchen." But she stays and sits down, settling in for a chat. Joe stands, as though on guard.

"Never thought we'd see you again," she says.

"I'm sorry it's been so long. Charlotte brought me, actually."

"When I heard you playing, I thought of your mother right off," Cora says. "We've never heard music like that here before or since. The girl with the violin, too! We're going to have the Pittsburgh Symphony here this summer. Concerts outdoors. If it works—we could become their summer home."

"If you all will excuse me," Joe says and limps away, a halt and hesitation in his gait. He walks like an old man.

Cora watches him leave with a worried look, lips pursed. She sighs and stands. "I should see how my girls are doing in the kitchen. But I'll see you at breakfast. We can really visit then." She gives me a quick, firm hug, and embraces Charlotte as well. "I always told Joe we should have made more of an effort to be in touch. I worried what happened to you. Losing your father. Neal. Grace. Goodness, just alone in the world." There's no edge to her words, just warmth. Cora bustles out of the room.

I feel a little dazed. Joe never told her. He's protected me, even with her.

"I thought Joe was your boyfriend, before I knew you were married," says Charlotte.

"My husband's best friend."

"And you never came back?" she asks.

"No."

She closes the keyboard.

"Nejiko Suwa played, the night before they left. Without your mother," I tell her.

"She tours, you know. Still has the violin. Controversial," Charlotte says.

We sit on the balcony outside our rooms, watching the bats swoop, listening to the owl. The moon rises over the forested mountainside across the road.

After she goes to bed, I'm restless. I wish I could call Ted. Fretting about school, stirred up by the day and memories, I wander downstairs, through the lobby, past the swimming pool, to the game room. Canned music hums from speakers hanging on the heavy mantelpiece above the huge rough fireplace. The room still smells smoky from years of winter fires. There are pin ball machines now, as well as the old ping pong table. I serve ball after ball across the net, listening to the hollow sound of the balls striking the floor and rolling away. If Joe would come, I could finally thank him, and apologize.

Upstairs, I find a large envelope slipped under the door to my room. It's addressed to Hazel Shaw, care of the Bedford Springs Hotel, Bedford, Pennsylvania, USA, in the round cursive of a child. The stamps are faded British stamps with frilly edges, postmarked January, 1946. On the reverse, written across the back flap, I read the return address: *Charlotte Harada, Greycotes School, Oxford, England.*

Paper-clipped to the envelope is a note on Bedford Springs letterhead.

Hazel. This came after you went. I held onto it, for when you came back.

So here it is. Joe.

It holds a few cut-paper snowflakes, frail and yellowed with age like old lace, and half a dozen drawings. I've seen my share of children's drawings at annual school art shows. For a thirteen year old girl, these are remarkable. Spare black pencil lines, with just accents of color: a hawk sailing over the ridge above the trees, two girls on a blue lake in a green canoe; a building engulfed in flames; her father's face; a bowl with gold seams.

> *Dear Hazel, You were my best and only friend in America.*
> *I have no friends here. I made these with the pencils you*
> *gave me, and used the crane scissors for the snowflakes.*
> *How is my father? Please write. Cha-chan.*

On the balcony, light shines through her curtains. She is still awake. I tap on the door. "It's me," I say, softly.

She's wrapped in a blue and white patterned cotton kimono—a *yukata*—like the violinist practiced in.

"Charlotte, I just saw these for the first time. I left before they came—I'm so sorry—you must have wondered …"

"I thought you had forgotten me—or written and my mother hid your letters."

She leafs through the drawings. She stops for a long moment at the drawing of her father.

"May I keep this one?" she asks.

"They're yours. But—I would like to have the one of the bowl."

She smoothes the creases in a paper snowflake. "I have the scissors, the bird scissors."

Before bed, I brush my hair in front of the mirror. I open the satin pouch and spill her mother's pearls into my hand. I should have returned them to her tonight, but I need to wear them to my meeting with Abel and Jacques on Monday. Borrow the charm for courage and dignity, one last time.

Cora sits with us at breakfast, curious, chattering.

"So you never re-married, Hazel? He was one in a million. Joe gave up fishing. Said it just wasn't the same without Neal. And running a school! Wouldn't your father be proud of you."

"Do you have children?" I ask.

"Our Neal died in Vietnam," she says.

I put my hand on hers.

After breakfast, Charlotte and I stand on the balcony and look out one last time at the mountainside, the pavilion, the forest, and the green expanse of the golf course.

Cora comes to the porch to see us off, alone. Driving away, I glance into the rear view mirror. Joe has joined her.

Charlotte waves until the hotel is out of sight.

"The Japanese way to say good-bye," I say.

"You remember!" Her eyes light with pleasure.

"Would you mind," I ask her, "if we took our time on the way back? There are a couple of places I'd like to see." I won't be back again.

"Of course not," she says.

We drive west out of town on Route 30 through Schellsburg. The village is unchanged except for a flashing stoplight by the bank. I continue on, up to the Ship.

The restaurant is shuttered and the doors are chained shut. It is so dilapidated it looks as though the next wind will pitch it down the mountainside.

The guard rail is broken. The valley spreads out beneath us. Mist is rising off the fields and forests below.

"It looks like the ocean," she says.

"The first one I ever saw."

A hawk soars by, so close it seems as though we could reach and touch its wings. Perhaps it's the one we saw yesterday on the drive up. Neal's spirit is watching, I think.

"That hawk has been following us," she says. "Your husband's spirit."

Startled by the moment of telepathy, I glance at her. She gazes out over the valley.

Returning down the mountainside, retracing our route through Schellsburg, I turn left at the stoplight and take the road towards Friend's Cove and the Dunning's Creek Meeting House. The tall brick building stands in the shade of the fir trees. The door is open. Meeting is in session. I park.

"It's the Quaker Meeting where my father and I went."

"I've never been."

"They've started already. I don't want to go inside—but my parents' graves are here."

"I'll wait."

"Come, please."

The windows of the Meeting House are placed high in the brick walls. No one inside will be distracted by us walking by. I remember sitting on a hard bench inside and watching the sky through rippled glass. The windows need washing, and putty.

The cemetery is mown and weeded.

I find my parents' simple stones. Gray-green lichen covers the surface. I've outlived them by so long. She was twenty, he was forty-five. I trace her dates: my birthday—her death day. A scattering of violets blooms in the grass.

"They were young," Charlotte says.

"She died having me. He had a heart attack."

"You were an only child?"

"The end of the line," I say. I balance a pebble on each stone. "A Jewish custom."

She adds a pebble to each marker. "Reminds me of the shrines to the babies in Kyoto."

Charlotte wanders further down the row of markers, leaving me alone with my parents. I wish I had a jam jar of flowers to leave. Help me tomorrow at school, I say to my father, help me to discern the right path.

I find her, standing in front of another marker.

"I like this inscription," she says, and reads aloud: "*They that love beyond the world cannot be separated by it. Death cannot kill what never dies. —William Penn.*"

We drive back through Bedford. I fill up at Dunkle's Gas and then drive up to the Jail, still guarding its corner. But the high wire fence behind the building is gone, and there is a banner fluttering from our front porch: "Antiques."

I pull to the curb. The curtains are closed in my bedroom windows. I remember the window seat, my perch and vantage point. One of the things about leaving a place behind is never again being inside looking out.

"We lived here. My father kept the jail." I don't need to defend him to her nor explain that he was fair and kind within the limits of his duty. We both know about our fathers.

The heft of the door knocker feels so familiar. An elderly woman answers. She's skinny, wearing jeans and a Bedford Bisons tee shirt—the football team, Neal's team. A small dingy-white dog barks fiercely from its safe position between her ankles.

"I don't really open till eleven on Sundays. Feel free to look around. Holler if you see anything you want. I'll be in the kitchen."

She's a good housekeeper. The wood is shining and I smell wax. How solid old buildings are, especially this one—a fortress built to last. The oak floor feels sturdier than any floor I've ever stood on since. I rest my hand on the square newel post of the banister, longing to go up.

Charlotte is sifting through a bowl of leather key fobs on a table by the door.

"These are from the Springs," she says. "Look! The Cottage. The Annex."

The dining room is crowded with tables laden with old china.

"I'm back here!" the woman calls out. The dog yaps from its hiding place under the kitchen table. She is standing at our deep double sink.

I'll wash, you dry, I hear my father say. This is the room he died in. This is the room where I sat by his elbow, learning to read as he taught a young inmate. This is the room where Neal and I did homework.

"I'd like these key fobs," Charlotte says.

"Dollar a piece. From the resort," she says. "Last time they renovated. You should go see it."

"Where's the jail now?" I ask.

"Way out of town," she says. "My late husband and I bought the place to turn it into an antiques mall with lots of vendors. Too much for me alone."

The heavy metal door to the cell block is standing open. We always kept it bolted, triple locked—except the night the high school burned.

"That's where they kept them. Like to see? The construction on this is really something," she says. "The cell block is riveted steel, like a ship, from Pittsburgh."

I've only been in this part of the building rarely, on Christmas, helping him deliver dinner and gifts.

It's bleaker than I recall, or maybe his presence warmed it. We peer into the two solitary cells and two larger ones with double bunks. There's a shower stall at the end of the passageway, incongruous pink and gray tiles from after our time.

"The Scouts wanted to use this for a haunted house last Halloween but I couldn't get a use permit," she says, cheerful.

Back outside, I blink in the bright sunlight and take a long breath of fresh air.

"Was it scary for you, living there?" asked Charlotte.

"My father wasn't afraid so neither was I. Quakers were always into prison reform. He said good people can do bad things, and learn to be better. He believed in the inner light in everyone."

"How do you handle discipline at a Quaker school?" Charlotte asks.

"Well, we have P & D, Procedures and Discipline. The Dean of Students runs it, with faculty and student representatives. I sit in, and have the final say."

"And what are the punishments?"

"Service hours, mostly, for small infractions, like breaking curfew," I say. "Though one of my teachers believes punishment should be meaningless and likes kids to copy pages out of the phone book."

"We had to walk laps around the hockey field," she says.

I remember her father, and the Ambassador, walking in circles on the hotel lawn like fish caught in a small pond.

"And with a serious infraction? What happens then?" she asks.

"Well, we have an honor code. Cheating—that results in suspension, even expulsion."

"Those must be difficult cases," she says.

"Yes."

I fall silent, thinking of Jacques, and Louisa, and tomorrow's meeting with Abel.

We drive back to Washington with the top down. The sun and the breeze take the place of conversation. The white marble of the Lincoln Memorial, the golden horses, gleam as we cross the bridge. The blossoms are deeper pink now, and the path around the Tidal Basin is packed.

"It's too crowded now, but I could come tomorrow evening and take you," I say.

"A blossom viewing," she says. "Lovely."

I pull up in front of her building.

"Thank you," she says, "for—everything."

"Thank you forever," I say.

"Come in for a drink?"

I'm tempted to stay, have a drink, and then another. I would like to hide here, postpone facing what is waiting for me at Clear Spring. But I must be clear and centered tomorrow. It's late, and I must discern my way.

"I have to get back," I say.

The repainted sign with its crisp, white letters reminds me of the very first time I turned onto the campus. I had immediately felt a sense of coming home. And ever since, after an absence of any length, I've turned onto the property with that same sensation of homecoming. But this time, I drive between the lush green playing fields—our treasure, our invaluable collateral—and feel dread rather than sanctuary.

I drop my suitcase in the foyer. The answering machine blinks, demanding my delinquent attention.

Abel has left several messages, increasingly insistent. *Call! We must speak as soon as possible.*

Sally doesn't sound like herself: my serene secretary's taped voice is on the edge of panic. *Call Abel right away. He's very upset with me, not knowing where you are. Dick Wilson has been calling. Where are you? Are you alright?*

Ted's voice is cheerful, teasing. *How was your trip down memory lane? Got our tickets for "Biloxi Blues." Time off for good behavior when school is out! Don't do anything rash. Except see me again.*

Jacques hasn't called.

I phone Sally first to apologize and reassure her. I am back, fine. Yes, I'll call Abel.

Abel sounds stern. "Where in creation have you been?"

"I'm sorry—a personal matter."

"Hell of a time to disappear." He never swears. "Dick Wilson called. He says he's pulling the trigger on a story in the *Post* if we don't fire Jacques immediately."

"He wouldn't want her exposed to publicity like that." But I'm really not sure. He's ruthless.

"Jacques called me. To resign," Abel says.

"You didn't accept?" I asked.

"No. But I could have. With your whereabouts unknown, I'm acting Head."

He's right. We both know the bylaws.

"I told him we were meeting with Jacques tomorrow. You must accept, Hazel."

"Dick's a bigoted bully. He wouldn't try this if Jacques were white."

"Hazel, this isn't about race. We're talking about the health of the school. About saving Jacques and his wife from a smear."

"It's about honor, Abel. Integrity. It's not good for the school, to give in to this."

"Don't put the school at risk—and yourself too."

Reminding me, gently reminding me, the Board hires and fires the Head.

"Please, Hazel," he says. "I have your back."

"I don't need you to protect me," I say. And then, "I'm sorry, Abel. See you tomorrow."

It's almost ten when I walk down the dark lane to the cluster of faculty houses beyond the pond. At the communal sandbox—where Jacques's baby should have a chance to play—I almost trip on an abandoned tricycle. Some of the resident faculty say we need brighter lighting at night, for security. But miles from the city, the stars brilliant above our campus, it has always felt safe. Until now.

Angelique answers the door, barefoot. Her eyelids are puffy. Following her into the house, I see the petite woman's swollen ankles beneath her loose robe. I try to embrace her. She stands stiff in my arms. I feel the swell of her belly.

Jacques enters, immaculate in pressed jeans and a white shirt. This is Jacques off duty—as close to informal as he ever gets.

She steps beside him, and they face me as though I am the enemy. Her eyes burn like hot coals.

"It's late, forgive me for disturbing you. But Abel told me. Please, Jacques. We can get through this. We must hold firm."

"Nothing can set this right. I will go to the meeting, Hazel, out of respect for protocol. But you must accept my resignation. We will move as soon as we can. Stay with friends."

"But—the baby, Angelique's dissertation—it's a terrible time to move."

"It would be worse to stay."

"Please," I say, "sleep on it."

"We're not sleeping much," he says.

I don't sleep, either. I would like to call Ted, but he is in bed with his wife, deeply embedded with his real responsibilities, in his real world. How thin what we have together is, how frivolous and selfish.

It seems I hear the clock chime every hour all night long. I'm wrestling with Spirit, my father would say, struggling to discern the Way. What is the honorable way through this, the right way out?

There's one that becomes clear, only one. And I do not like it.

Very early, as soon as it is light, I walk through the woods along the paths that were once travelled by fugitive slaves on the Underground Railway. I reach the Meeting House. The broad white double door is kept locked now. I sit on the porch bench, listening to the familiar creaks and sighs of the old building—a soft chorus approving my reluctant decision.

Back at home, I dress carefully for the meeting with Abel and Jacques, in my gray silk suit. I clasp Gwendolyn's pearls around my neck—borrowing their charm for courage, one last time. I wear my opal ring and touch Neal's photograph for strength.

Abel is already in my office. He's sitting in the same captain's chair where Dick Wilson sat. My friend, my wise counselor, rises and hugs me, the consoling embrace given in defeat. He is not going to fight for Jacques. He has had no change of heart.

"A sad morning," he says. "You've come to terms with this? Discerned what's necessary?"

"Yes." I lean against his broad shoulder for a moment longer. It would have been good, would be good, to have someone fully in my life, in the way Ted can never be. But it's a lonely valley, as the spiritual goes. You have to walk it by yourself.

We sit in silence, waiting.

Jacques enters, regal and dignified. No wonder the lonely girl fixed on him. I understand how that happens.

He offers me the envelope. His eyes are luminous. "My resignation."

There is a pause, a breath-held moment.

"You're sure?" I ask. "You know my mind. You know I want you to stay."

He nods.

I take the envelope. It is heavy in my hands, like the War Department envelope forty years ago. "I only accept at your request."

"Thank you," he says.

"We will of course provide you our highest recommendation," says Abel, holding out his hand. The two men shake and Jacques starts to leave.

"Wait, please," I say. "There is something I want you both to know."

Both look at me, intent. I hesitate. Hold the mended bowl of my life aloft, poised to smash it down. And then it's time. "I am resigning as well."

They speak almost at once.

"I cannot accept that," says Abel.

"Not on my account," says Jacques.

"I must. It is—a matter of honor."

Jacques leaves. His footsteps echo down the corridor, down the stairs. The door of the building slams closed.

"I will see the school year out. Help you find an interim head."

"This is hasty, Hazel. Ill-considered."

"I am called to do this. And now, it's time to go to the barn, for Meeting. Join me?"

Ted calls, just before lunch. "So?"

"He resigned, I accepted."

"You had to, Hazel. It was the right thing to do."

"Not right. Expedient."

"You know what I meant."

"I resigned, too, Ted."

"Don't be a fool. Abel will never accept it."

"He did. No one is indispensable."

"Take it back. Reconsider. Why didn't you talk to me first?"

"How and when could I do that?"

"Hazel—I have that open history slot."

"You know that's impossible."

His secretary is calling him. That's how it is, for us; other needs must take priority. We say good-bye. I'm almost sure that it is not just my job that is ending. He has his responsibilities, his loyalties. There are after all, matters of honor. Higher authorities, my father would say.

And then my own day claims me. I have a substitute French teacher to find.

It is almost nine that evening when I pick Charlotte up for our visit to the cherry blossoms. The crowd has thinned to lingering sweethearts and the park police. Starting at the massive stone lantern, we walk halfway around the Tidal Basin under the canopy of flowering branches. The blossoms are magical at night, the essence of snow.

"The Japanese would call this a *hanami*," she says. "A flower viewing party. To celebrate the season."

We stop and sit on the steps of the Jefferson Memorial. Across the water, the stark spire of the Washington Monument splits the sky, and its reflection falls into the basin. Water laps at the edge of the vast marble bowl.

"The tide is going out," she says. "Does it ever flood here?"

"We have hurricanes, occasionally. Washington is a reclaimed swamp."

"Fitting, for Japanese trees to be vulnerable. Over there it's always something—volcanoes, tsunamis. Bombs."

"After Pearl Harbor, women protected these trees from vigilantes."

The moon's reflection floats in the water. I touch the pearls, her mother's pearls, for courage. "Charlotte, when I learned about my husband—I turned to your father, imposed myself on him."

"What are you saying?"

"I demanded he comfort me."

"You and he?" Her voice sounds lost, like a child's.

"I shamed him. I'm to blame for what he did—with me, and—the next morning."

She sits still and silent for what seems like a very long time, then sighs. "You told me I can't claim responsibility for his death. So neither can you." There's anger in her tone: at him, at me, at herself.

I unclasp the pearls. "These are your mother's," I say. "She left them with me. They've given me strength in difficult times."

It is too dark to see her expression clearly. She holds up her hair, bows her head. I fasten the strand around her neck. We sit silent, watching the tide flow out. Out, out, out with the water.

The evening breeze freshens, wrinkling the gray satin water, stirring up a verdant scent. We proceed around the basin, passing one of the oldest trees, so severely pruned it resembles a valiant amputee. Gnarled and asymmetrical, its trunk is protected from beaver by a mesh cage. "This is one of the originals given to Mrs. Taft," I say.

"They prop old trees up in Japan. Honor them as venerated elders."

"This tree wrapped in wire reminds me—there's a sculpture dedicated to the Nisei internees on Capitol Hill. A crane trapped in barbed wire. I'll show you one day."

She strokes the tree's corrugated bark. Bracts of blooms scatter along the trunk of the crippled tree in defiance of age and frailty.

"My father used to say what is broken is beautiful," she says.

"I remember," I say.

We complete our walk around the Basin as the tide flows out to the Potomac. Blossoms drift down like snow. We walk quietly, remembering.

Remembering, simply remembering, must serve as my confession. And letting go must approximate forgiveness.

Out with the water. Out with the water.

End

Reading Group Guide

The Bowl with Gold Seams

Ellen Prentiss Campbell

Questions for Discussion

1. How did Hazel's Quaker upbringing shape her outlook on life and how she interacted with others? Do you think that Hazel's father's credo that if you are doing right "ask forgiveness not permission" is a good code to follow?

2. Describe the climate of animosity in which the Japanese detainees found themselves during their internment at the Bedford Springs Hotel. Do you agree with Hazel when she turns to Joe and says (p. 94), "Hating everyone Japanese is like something Hitler would have done"?

3. Which characters in this novel resonated most with you? Did you find that cultural, geographic, or social differences among the characters made them difficult to relate to?

4. When Hazel tries to return Gwendolyn Harada's pearls and Gwendolyn refuses them for either herself or for Charlotte, Gwendolyn looks at Hazel in anger and says, "My daughter must forget him." Why do you think she feels that way?

5. What made Hazel notice Takeo Harada, Charlotte's father, and feel drawn to him? Why did he play such a pivotal role in her personal story and in the novel? Why do you think he chose to

commit suicide?

6. How does Hazel view her younger self and her choices and actions? Does that view change upon meeting Charlotte again later in life?

7. While driving to the Bedford Springs Hotel together, Charlotte asks Hazel about her Peace Studies course (p. 182) and the people who come to speak about their war experiences. Hazel mentions a Quaker conscientious objector who served as a medic in Germany and was with the troops that liberated Buchenwald. He tells Hazel's students "... after seeing the camp and the survivors, he lost his belief in pacifism. That what he saw was so evil he wished he'd fought against it." What impact might that have on Hazel's students? What impact does it have on you?

8. When Hazel and Charlotte visit the hotel and take a swim in the pool where Mia had drowned, Charlotte says (p. 193), "This is a pilgrimage, isn't it? A way of trying to let the past go. To let it go. Out with the water." What about each of their pasts are they trying to let go? How do they hope to change their paths forward by letting go?

9. Have you ever had to go back to the past to move forward in the future?

10. Why does Hazel have so much difficulty in returning to Charlotte the strand of pearls and the bowl with the gold seams? What significance do these objects hold for Hazel? What effect does returning these objects have on Hazel? On Charlotte?

11. How did the losses that Hazel and Charlotte experienced as children impact the choices they made as adults? Were there positive outcomes of those experiences?

12. What is the significance of Hazel's career as an educator at a Quaker School? What connection do you see between her choice of profession and her experience as a child and as a young woman during the war?

13. Why has Hazel kept her wartime experience secret? How has keeping this secret impacted her life?

14. What is the significance of the title? How does the theme of mended damage figure in the book? How does the bowl with gold seams represent Hazel and Charlotte's experiences of love and loss?

15. When Hazel tells Ted that she has resigned (p. 211) and says goodbye to him when his secretary interrupts their call, she says to herself, "I'm almost sure that it is not just my job that is ending." What in her life might be ending? What in her life might be beginning? What do you imagine Hazel may do after the conclusion of the book?

About the Author

Ellen Prentiss Campbell is the author of the short story collection *Contents Under Pressure*. Her short fiction has been featured in numerous journals including *The Massachusetts Review, The American Literary Review*, and *The Southampton Review*. Essays and reviews appear in *The Fiction Writers Review*, where she is a contributing editor, and *The Washington Independent Review of Books*. A graduate of The Bennington Writing Seminars and the Simmons School of Social Work, she is a practicing psychotherapist. In both her writing and her clinical work she seeks the story between the lines and behind the words. Campbell lives with her husband in Washington, D.C., and summers in Manns Choice, Pennsylvania—near the Bedford Springs Hotel.

Connect online at ellencampbell.net.

Apprentice House is the country's only campus-based, student-staffed book publishing company. Directed by professors and industry professionals, it is a nonprofit activity of the Communication Department at Loyola University Maryland.

Using state-of-the-art technology and an experiential learning model of education, Apprentice House publishes books in untraditional ways. This dual responsibility as publishers and educators creates an unprecedented collaborative environment among faculty and students, while teaching tomorrow's editors, designers, and marketers.

Outside of class, progress on book projects is carried forth by the AH Book Publishing Club, a co-curricular campus organization supported by Loyola University Maryland's Office of Student Activities.

Eclectic and provocative, Apprentice House titles intend to entertain as well as spark dialogue on a variety of topics. Financial contributions to sustain the press's work are welcomed. Contributions are tax deductible to the fullest extent allowed by the IRS.

To learn more about Apprentice House books or to obtain submission guidelines, please visit www.apprenticehouse.com.

Apprentice House
Communication Department
Loyola University Maryland
4501 N. Charles Street
Baltimore, MD 21210
Ph: 410-617-5265 • Fax: 410-617-2198
info@apprenticehouse.com • www.apprenticehouse.com

CPSIA information can be obtained
at www.ICGtesting.com
Printed in the USA
FFOW04n2121180816
26767FF